The Benevolence
of New Ideas

Other books by Carmela Cattuti:

Between the Cracks:
One Woman's Journey from Sicily to America

The Ascent

The Benevolence of New Ideas

Carmela Cattuti

Three Towers Press
Milwaukee, Wisconsin

Published by
Three Towers Press
An imprint of HenschelHAUS Publishing, Inc.
Milwaukee, Wisconsin 53220
www.henschelHAUSbooks.com

ISBN: 978159598-869-0
E-ISBN: 978159598-870-6
LCCN: 2021947911

Printed in the United States of America.

*"When I thought I couldn't go on,
I forced myself to keep going.
My success is based on persistence, not luck."*

—Estee Lauder

To William Duane Hess,
who got me this far.

TABLE OF CONTENTS

Preface

The Transition

Angela sat by her husband's hospital bed and waited for the end to come. She wondered how she should move forward in her life after Franco took his last breath. He had married and brought her from Sicily in 1913 and now, years later, he lay dying from a stroke. In life he constantly expressed his opinion, regardless of popular sentiment, and now his voice was gone; his shallow breathing was the last functioning system. He had had several strokes over the years, this was the one that would take his life. Angela had sat with many of her family members and friends during the past decades as they transitioned into the next world: her mother-in-law, sister-in-law, and older Italian immigrants who left their homeland and never saw the land of their birth again.

Franco's chest rose slowly and fell abruptly, as if his lungs were attempting to perform their function but the soul who had inhabited the body had already vacated and was waiting for his lungs to stop so he could complete the process and move on. When Franco executed his final breath, Angela anxiously awaited his next inhale—but his chest was still. He had gone.

Angela had cared for Franco during his long illness, and now she was free. The relief she felt made her cringe. How could she so easily feel relief when Franco had suffered? She grieved but was thankful there would be no more concerns about leaving him home alone, or trips to the doctor, or Franco insisting he could perform a task when he couldn't. He had emigrated from Sicily at age twelve 12 in the early 20th century full of energy and promise. Now, in 1968, Angela looked back and felt he had been successful in fulfilling that promise. Franco had brought Angela, at age eighteen, from the convent orphanage in Palermo, where she had lived since the 1908 earthquake, to a new life in Nelsonville, New York, about forty -five minutes north of Manhattan. It was not the life she thought she would have in America, but what she had created in America she never would have had the opportunity to experience had she stayed in Sicily.

Angela kissed Franco several times on both cheeks and on the lips. The doctors had said it was a matter of time until he would pass away. She could see death hovering and begin to slowly drape his body from his head to his feet as if giving Angela time to say good-bye.

"*Adio mio caro*," whispered Angela. "*Grazie di tutto.*" Tears rolled down her face onto Franco's cheek and mouth. His eyes were open and fixed, as if peering into the world beyond. She put her hands on the sides of his face and with her thumbs closed his eyes. A nurse stepped into the room.

"He's gone," said Angela.

Angela gathered her pocketbook and scarf, went to the door, and stepped over the threshold. The nurse had covered Franco's body with a sheet as if to close a chapter on a life. The 1960s were ending, and so was Angela's former life and attitudes.

Chapter 1

THE NEXT GENERATION, 1968

"**A**ngela, how are you doing with Franco gone?" asked Sadie Malaci. She sipped her coffee and crossed her legs, her ankles so swollen that her elastic stockings bulged at her ankles. Few people asked her how she was feeling since Franco's death, so it was difficult to answer. There was an inevitability of death, and when it happened one embraced it as God's will and part of life. Angela had experienced many death scenarios from violent to peaceful. The violent deaths she saw during the earthquake in Messina in 1908 and the quiet death of her sister-in-law, Speranza, from heart failure were opposite ends of the death spectrum. The time leading up to Franco's death was a struggle, but when she thought of his last moments, she remembered his peace. Still, she felt he had left the earth with unfinished business.

"I'm fine. You know he worked his whole life but got little. He was too generous with people. He should have charged more for his services," I said.

"As long as he had all those properties for income, I guess he didn't have to charge so much," said Sadie, sipping her coffee. "I seem to remember you have been generous with people too. You gave away your furniture to a newly arrived couple from Sicily, and you visited everyone in the Italian community who was sick. Raised your sister-in-law's children and now Nunzio's. Should I go on?"

"No, I do what I feel is right. Besides, I benefit too; it makes me stronger. When I came to this country, I was weak, but now I can contribute."

"I don't think you were ever weak."

"I suppose," said Angela. "Franco collected rents for many years and then sold the houses."

"Well, that's good for you," said Sadie.

"Yes, and I am blessed with Felicia and the kids living here."

"They were the second generation born in this country," said Sadie. "It gets easier as future generations are born."

"I guess we had to find our place," said Angela.

In Sicily, there was a rigid social structure. People kept to their own social group or place in society. Angela's father was of the merchant class, so all social activities revolved around other merchant families. In America, there appeared to be a fluid social structure, but there was still a framework.

"How's the family?" Sadie asked.

"Very well. Felicia and Marie visited Joe in Manhattan not too long ago," said Angela.

"It's good that generations get to live together," said Sadie. "People get to share what life was like for them. We all pave the way for each other."

"I have never regretted leaving Sicily when I did. I avoided two world wars there," said Angela. "It was clear that I was to leave."

"You didn't agonize over it?" asked Sadie.

"I did, but the Blessed Mother told me that I should take a chance, so I did."

"You came to the new world because Mary the mother of God told you to? I thought you came because your family was killed in the earthquake and you didn't want to become a nun."

"That is also true, but I know this is where I am supposed to be," said Angela.

"So, you talk with spirits you can't see and take advice?" asked Sadie.

"What do you mean?"

"I know you still talk to your sister-in-law Speranza and other people who have passed over," said Sadie. "Who else do you talk to?"

"Should this be any of your business?" asked Angela.

"Nah, I guess not," said Sadie. "Talk away if you like. We Italians like to say we mind our own business, but we both know we're also nosey."

Angela laughed and changed the subject. Sadie had been Angela's friend for many years, and they shared many secrets, but Angela had never told Sadie about her unseen spirit friends. Angela thought it best to keep her spirit friends to herself. It was her secret weapon, her way of connecting with her deeper self and utilizing the information to benefit herself and other people.

"I need to be on my way," said Sadie. "My daughter is coming by this afternoon."

Angela sipped espresso in her kitchen on Morning Glory Avenue. She looked out of her window into the garden and admired her ripening tomatoes and other vegetables. Her husband had been dead for a few months, and she remembered how he loved to turn the soil over for spring planting. Angela thought there would come a time when there would be no garden and that weeds would cover the soil.

Felicia, Angela's nephew Nunzio's widow, and her great-nieces and nephews lived upstairs, and she could not be happier. When Angela and Franco bought the house on Morning Glory Avenue, the second floor was a shell of potential to Angela. She visualized her family living and thriving upstairs, taking advantage of all America had to offer. Unable to bear children, Angela had wanted to adopt a child, but Franco was opposed. In hindsight, she saw that she was needed, first by her sister-in-law, Speranza's children, and then by her nephew Nunzio's children, all of which softened the blow of being childless. Her unseen friends told her that her mission was different from the women she knew.

Nunzio's early death still loomed over the family dynamics, but it was not discussed. No one talked about Nunzio's effect on the family, nor did it seem like he was missed. He had lived most of his life in the house on Morning Glory Avenue, he'd been gone for ten years, and people carried on. Felicia had decided to continue living on Morning Glory Avenue with Angela after Nunzio's death, and when Angela awoke every morning, she was still heartened by the flurry of activity coming from upstairs. Felicia had gone into the workforce and found employment at as an office manager at a real estate title company. She was now so valued and successful that the owner had her doing closings on houses. Closings on homes were usually done by male attorneys, so whenever Felicia showed up, the other attorney was usually disgruntled that a woman was doing the closing.

Angela had helped Felicia create a stable home for the children. Even though she was a single mother, she had had assistance and support from Angela and Franco; the children did not have to want for anything and there was always someone in the house when the children returned from school. It was an extended family situation that worked.

When Angela first came to America, her sister-in-law, Speranza, was nine years old and in need of a mother figure. Childless herself, Angela filled that role, and when Speranza died at the age of twenty-eight, Angela and Franco had raised her children. Angela had been angered by Speranza's choice of a husband, Salvatore, who had infantile paralysis and did not have a trade to support a family. The marriage was arranged by his sister Paolina, so Angela had blamed Salvatore and Paolina for Speranza's ensuing ill health.

As a new American citizen, Angela was determined to integrate into her new situation but was also resolute about being herself. This was more important than culture or social class, it was about her essence. As the years passed and she became more connected to American culture, the unseen spirit world became more accessible and she began to walk between the worlds.

When Angela had arrived in the United States, America was a young country that looked to the future instead of the past. Despite its youth, America had become a major power in the world.

The Italian-American community had integrated into mainstream America at a rapid rate. Angela had experienced America's underbelly during the early 20th century—war, dark money, and political corruption—and now it was time to collect on America's promise of freedom and equality. Angela was adept at navigating the changing American landscape. Felicia had provided the practical aspects of life to her children, but Angela provided them the vision.

She cleared the table and began to rearrange the pictures on the fireplace mantle. She liked to move pictures of family around; it was as if she gained a new perspective on events and relationships. She put pictures of her great-nieces and -nephews next to their grandmother Speranza. They had never met, but it was as if they were having a relationship.

She then straightened pictures on the dining room buffet. There was one of her nephew, Nunzio and his wife Felicia and their two boys, Robert and Frank, taken in the backyard many years ago. Nunzio was the only one not smiling. He had a beautiful family, Angela thought, but he did not look happy. A photograph of Speranza's children, Nunzio, Alicia, and Joe, sat beside the crystal bowl, taken when they were young. Nunzio stuck his tongue out at the camera, while Joe stood behind and held up his index and middle finger over his brother's head. Alicia sat with legs crossed and her hands placed demurely in her lap. In another photo, Felicia's daughters, Marie and Andrea, curtsied with wide-brimmed straw hats and flowered dresses.

A picture of Franco was beside the family photo, showing his full mustache, slicked back hair, and a suit and tie—all the accoutrements of style and success in the world. She had come to America fifty-five years ago, but she found as she grew older that distant memories seemed to move closer to the present. They did not want to die out with Angela; they wanted to be passed on.

Angela remembered her father's funeral and how the priest talked about the need for more protection for silk traders who traveled the precarious silk trade road. Her father had been a trader and was robbed and killed along the silk trade route. The merchants encountered many hardships, hot deserts, cold snowy mountains, and many marauding tribes who stole their wares. The fragility of life was stamped in Angela's conscious-ness on the day her father was lost to a bandit's bullet. She had learned that physical safety was a prerequisite to surviving the unpredictable terrain of life.

The day Franco walked into the convent in Palermo when she was seventeen, she knew that she had to take a chance. She had to dive into whatever was presented to her so she could live life. Franco had been living in the United States from the age of twelve and when it was time to marry, he had sought a bride in his native city of Palermo, Sicily. When Angela first saw Franco at the convent in 1912, he was dressed in a suit with a fedora and gold pocket watch. When they could meet, he presented a dapper image that drew Angela to him. He was well versed in Italian, Sicilian, and English. He seemed to love his family and took good care of them. Little did Angela know that when she arrived in America, he would expect her to care for his mother. Arriving in America, she had encountered a different life than she had expected.

Franco and Angela returned to Messina in 1929 to search for her sister, who had gone missing during the earthquake, but there were no records of her death, birth, or survival. Most of the records were lost during the eruption, and those who perished left no footprint that they ever lived. Still, the idea that she might have survived plagued Angela to this day in 1968.

During that visit, Angela had gone to the area where her house once stood, and in that space a new apartment building had been built. She went to another area of the city where, she remembered that through her communication with her unseen friends a few days after the earthquake, she had helped someone. She was only thirteen at the time. It was the same day she had found her brother, and they were walking with other children searching for their parents. They came upon a man who was kneeling in what used to be his home. He was crying and pointing to a pile of stone that was once the walls of his house. He was pleading with God to let his wife live.

"My wife is under here. Can you help me dig her out?" His eyes were wild with agony and his entreaties became more agitated.

A familiar inner voice told Angela to look up. Part of the ceiling was dangling over the man's head by a thin piece of metal.

"*Signore*, you need to leave this place," said Angela. "It is dangerous. The ceiling will fall on you."

"I cannot leave my wife," said the man. "My wife will die."

"She is already dead," Angela said. "Please move away from here."

The ceiling creaked and the man looked up. His eyes widened.

Angela grabbed the man's arm and, with the help of the other children, pulled him to safety. The ceiling fell where his wife was entombed. They escorted the grieving man back to the American rescue ships. Angela recognized the inner voice as one of her unseen friends. She had had a connection with voices from spirits since she was a child, and as she matured so did her communication abilities.

At seventy-three, Angela was still designing dresses for clients and her great-nieces. When she first came to America, she sewed linens for St. Mary's Episcopal School and faced ridicule from her co-workers who were less detailed about their work. The nuns wanted the other workers to produce the same quality linens that Angela produced, but they did not have her skill. They felt their jobs were in jeopardy, so they would not eat lunch with her. Angela spoke little English, but she knew they were saying unkind things.

"She thinks she's superior to us because she's European," said one of the women. "But the nuns will see through that."

"She will make double work for us," said another. "Those designs will take us hours. If we don't talk to her maybe she will leave."

Angela continued to do superior work regardless of being ostracized. When she learned enough English, she decided to start a dressmaking business where she could sew for whom she wanted.

Today Angela was looking forward to a fitting for her great-niece Marie, still asleep upstairs. She delighted chatting with sixteen-year-old Marie and hearing her modern feminine sensibility and determination. Angela put her cup in the sink when the doorbell rang. She looked out of the hall window and saw two tall men in trench coats and fedoras. Were they insurance salesman?

"Sorry to bother you, Ma'am. We are from the FBI," said one of the men. Both men took out their badges in a manner that was so synchronized they seemed like robots.

"What?" Angela asked. "Why are you here?"

In Sicily it did not bode well if the police came to your house. For over fifty years, she and Franco had avoided the authorities by ensuring that everything they did from paying taxes to parking was legitimate.

"We'd like to ask you about your nephew, Robert. He registered for the military draft, and then he disappeared. We are looking for him."

Angela's stomach turned. She and Marie were the only people in the house on this summer Monday morning. She wiped her sweaty hands on her apron. She didn't think she'd have to deal with another war after World War II ended. Marie's father, Nunzio, had come back from the Pacific theater a stranger. From the day he came home from the war until he died in 1958 from a heart attack, Angela felt that his soul had left his body and what was left was non-functioning. Everyone had been quiet about the change in Nunzio, not because they didn't want to talk about it, but because they didn't know if they should. She did not want his son, Robert, to suffer the same fate in Vietnam.

"I will get my great-niece, Robert's sister. She will be able to talk to you better than I can."

Angela fled upstairs into Marie's bedroom, where she was sound asleep.

She talked while she shook Marie awake.

"Wake up, wake up—the government police are downstairs looking for your brother."

"What?" asked Marie, wiping her eyes.

"The government police are here asking about Robert."

"Tell them we don't know where Robert is," said Marie. She rolled over on her side.

"This is serious," said Angela. "Please come downstairs and talk to them. They make me nervous."

Marie threw off her covers and followed her aunt downstairs.

"This is my great-niece," said Angela. "She can tell you we don't know where he is."

"We don't know where he is," said Marie.

Angela noticed that both men were the same height, had clear blue eyes, and wore the same red ties. It looked like they had stepped out of play.

Angela suddenly stepped back from the two men. They looked oddly familiar to her. A distant memory began to surface, one that she had tucked away for decades. After closer observation, she remembered a man she had encountered after the 1908 earthquake in Messina. He had been immaculately dressed in a dark blue suit with a trench coat resting over his arm. He too had fair skin and clear blue eyes and held a fedora in his hands. Most people had not washed in days and were filthy, including herself. He did not experience the earthquake, Angela had thought at the time. He had come out of nowhere.

"What are you looking for, little girl?" asked the man. He was standing in what was left of Angela's home.

"I am seeking my family," said Angela. She stepped away from the man.

"There is no one left," said the stranger. "Come with me, I'll help you find your family."

Angela had turned, run a few feet, and glanced over her shoulder. The man had disappeared. She had filed the incident away as a dream, but maybe it wasn't.

"You haven't heard from him at all?" asked one of the FBI men.

"No, I've been busy lately," said Marie, thinking that the men could be in a *Twilight Zone* episode.

"We'd like to use your phone," said one of the men.

"Over here," said Angela.

They seemed mannequin-like to Angela. As the agent dialed, she noticed his hands were manicured and his skin was so smooth that it appeared transparent. The agent noticed Angela watching his hands as he dialed, so he turned his back and shielded the phone.

"You realize that we will have to keep looking for him," said the other man.

"Well, if you find him, let us know where he is," said Marie. "He owes me $10."

Angela pinched Marie's arm.

"Well, he does," said Marie.

"He said he doesn't want to kill people," said Angela. She was wringing her hands.

"You're upsetting my aunt," said Marie. She knew that immediately after the agents left, Angela would get on the phone with her friends and broadcast what had transpired. That meant that Marie's dress fitting would be delayed, and she would miss her horseback riding time. She enjoyed her summer riding and her time on the beach. One glitch like this and her day would fall apart. She resented that the Vietnam War interfered with her summer. The war seemed to seep into the energy in the household and infect every nuance like a disease—except there was no cure.

Marie would often think about how she might use her talents in the future. She was influenced by her aunt and had developed Angela's intuition, able to anticipate events or know how someone's choices would turn out in the end. Marie thought that she might study history in college, since it had to do with past events and how they influenced the future.

"Here is my card," said one of the agents. "Let us know if you hear from him."

"Sure," said Marie. They're like characters in a bad B movie, she thought as they turned and left.

Angela drew in a deep breath and became animated. "Go upstairs and get dressed. I need to make some phone calls."

"But I need to get going. I'm supposed to be horseback riding this morning. I'll be late."

"If you want a new dress, then you will have to wait until I'm done talking on the phone."

Angela dialed her friend Sadie's phone number, hoping that she hadn't already had her first glass of wine.

"Hi, Angie. What are you doing?" asked Sadie.

"How did you know it was me?"

"No one else calls me on a Monday morning."

Angela and Sadie had been friends for many years and felt the same on many issues. Sadie lifted Angela's spirits with her forthright attitude toward everything. There was no subject for which Sadie did not hold a deep irreverence.

"We just had the FBI government police here looking for Robert. I'm so afraid that something bad will happen."

"They come by all the time when someone dodges the draft," said Sadie. "I would ignore them."

"They said we have to call them if we find out where he is. If we don't tell them, they can put us in jail," said Angela.

Marie came down the stairs dressed in frayed bell-bottom jeans and a peasant top. Angela assessed Marie's garb.

"Sadie, hold on a minute," said Angela.

"Marie, why are you dressed like a poor person?" asked Angela.

"I'm not dressed like a poor person. This is what everyone is wearing. And by the way, no one will send you to jail because you don't tell them where Robert is."

"Don't go out of the house looking like that," Angela said. "Take off those jeans and I will press and hem them."

"Since I'm not having the fitting, I want to go riding."

"You see what I struggle with, Sadie,' said Angela. "I try to make her presentable, but she doesn't listen."

Angela had spent her life as a fine fashion dressmaker, and if someone Angela knew saw Marie dressed like that she would be mortified. She had made Marie's clothing since she was an infant, and she loved the way Marie looked in her designs—feminine with structure. The world was changing, and so was women's daily wear. Women no longer had time to fuss with ruffles, slips, and girdles.

Ever since Marie had become a teenager, she wanted to assert her independence and make her own choices. Angela understood this but urged Marie to develop her own identity and not go along with the crowd. Maybe that's why she's comfortable wearing cutoff jeans, thought Angela.

When Marie was a baby, she had blonde hair and light skin—different from her siblings' black hair and olive skin. Angela had snipped a piece and kept it in her bureau. She had felt a strong connection to Marie from the very beginning.

Different than her siblings, who preferred to be out with their friends and participate in extracurricular activities at school, Marie spent hours with Angela. Marie's innate, intuitive sensibility was supported and developed by Angela. Marie attended the local public school and was counting the days until she could go to college and live in Manhattan. She was aiming for early acceptance in 1969 after her junior year.

"Sadie, I have to go. She is going to go out in those clothes," said Angela. She hung up and followed Marie into the kitchen.

"Where are you going looking like that?" Angela asked Marie.

"I'm supposed to go horseback riding, but now I'm going to be late."

Marie picked up a roll Angela had just taken out of the oven and bit into it. "Yum, I love your bread, Aunt Angela."

"I don't like that you're wearing those frayed jeans."

"No one cares if I'm wearing cutoff jeans when I'm riding."

"Don't you wear riding pants?" asked Angela.

"I'm riding at a dude ranch. We don't even wear helmets."

"I don't know what to think about your brother. I worry at night," said Angela. "What if the military police catch him?"

"Aunt Angela, this isn't World War ll. People don't want this war because it isn't about patriotism; it's about money and control. They would not give Robert a 4F classification, so he left. He's probably in Canada. He'll be fine."

Nobody wants to talk, thought Angela. Avoidance seemed to be the direction of the American culture, even with all the free love, protests, and self-expression by young people. With Franco gone and Felicia occupied with work and the children, Angela relied more on her friends and Marie for meaningful connection. When Angela came to America it was the new world, but now it was evolving into something else. It was unrecognizable to her now, and she was going to have to reinvent herself according to all the changes.

Angela thought about her dressmaking client, Sarah Einbinder, and her view on World War II. Sarah's view was that young men had been deceived into fighting for a hidden purpose. Angela was fitting Sarah for a dress the day Pearl Harbor was bombed, and her own views on America and war were changed forever on that day. Sarah believed that Henry Ford sold war vehicles to the Nazis.

"No war is good, not even World War II," Angela said to Marie.

"But people wanted to go to war to stop the Nazis," said Marie. "They were killing Jews, and Hitler had to be stopped."

"You know Mrs. Einbinder?" asked Angela.

"Your client? Yes," Marie mumbled with a mouthful of bread.

"Don't eat standing up; you'll get indigestion. And don't talk with your mouth full," said Angela. "Sit over here." Angela pulled out a chair and put out a plate and some butter.

Marie was used to her aunt's idiosyncrasies and would sometimes indulge her. At times, she found Angela exasperating, but she always knew when her aunt wanted her to expand her thinking. Marie looked at the time and decided her morning horseback ride was lost.

"When your father enlisted, I was against it," said Angela. "I felt he was too young, but he did it without our knowledge. What could I do? Like now, there was nothing we could do about the draft. I just wanted to tell you that sometimes things are not what they seem. This war in Vietnam is no different than any other. It will all end the same."

"What does this have to do with me? I'm not going to be drafted."

"I am just telling you what I experienced," Angela said. "Now take those jeans off so I can mend them."

Marie knew that Angela would hound her until she allowed her to sew and press her jeans, so she obliged.

"I need them soon. Maybe I can ride this afternoon."

"First I have to fit you for that dress. I should call your mother at the office and let her know about the FBI men."

"Call her later," said Marie. "There's nothing she can do. She doesn't know where Robert is."

Felicia was angry about her son's situation. He had grown his hair long and smoked a lot of pot and embraced the counterculture. It was not that she disagreed with the antiwar movement; she did not like the chaos it brought to the family. When Marie skipped school to horseback ride or go into Manhattan, she did not mind. "Do what you want but just don't get caught," she would say. "I will not come to your aid—I have enough to do." Felicia believed that people should do what they wanted but should not talk about it, and they must accept the consequences if things go wrong.

"In the end, the war killed your father."

"You told me that before," said Marie. Angela repeated stories from the past so often that Marie had them all memorized. When Marie was a child, she loved to hear stories about Sicily and the earthquake and how Angela met and married

Franco. She would describe the scenes from the 1908 earthquake in Messina to Marie in detail. It was epic, and Marie thought of her great aunt as a strong survivor who had come to America and built a dressmaking business from the ground up, in a new country, while not knowing the language or culture.

"This is my niece, Marie," Angela would say when she introduced her to her clients. "She is doing well and will go to college." She would beam when she said it, and Marie hoped she lived up to her great aunt's praise. Angela expected her to do great things and wanted to share with Marie her experience of taking risks and connecting with the unseen world.

Truthfully, Angela's stories had expanded Marie's interest in the world and made her question why things are as they are. Marie felt they were her stories now, too. Her aunt's repetitive stories about survival gave Marie confidence, but with her friends she was quiet and did not share the wisdom she had gleaned from her aunt. This tended to make her vulnerable to others' opinions. As Marie grew, Angela's influence became more apparent.

When Marie was in seventh grade at the local Catholic school, the nun had assigned the students to write an essay on how to communicate with God and follow His divine direction. Marie was enthusiastic about the assignment and naively shared some of her otherworldly experiences. In her essay she did not use the word God but took on her aunt's sensibility of expanding awareness and communicating with the unseen. Choice was also a theme she explored. She suggested that one could either accept or reject the communication, depending on the person's evaluation of the message.

"Marie, you have not mentioned God in your essay," said the nun. "You also talked about rejecting the communication and left it up to the receiver to decide if it was valid. God's word is law. This is unacceptable. I am sorry but I have no other option but to give you an F."

"But I spent a lot of time writing that essay," said Marie.

"If you would like to rewrite it with the appropriate view, then I would reconsider my decision."

"I stand by my essay. The messages come from the spiritual unseen realm. That is part of God." Marie held firm, but she found she was breathing heavily.

"You have no idea who is giving you guidance. It could be the devil," said the nun.

"It is not the devil. It is divine connection. Anyone can do it. My aunt does it."

"Don't be recalcitrant. You give me no choice but to inform your mother about your belligerence. She should be instructing you at home regarding Catholic doctrine."

When the nun phoned Marie's home, Angela was on the receiving end.

"I see, Sister. Marie has an active imagination, and I am sure she will be a writer one day. I try my best to encourage independent thinking. I don't see why she should receive an F."

"Mrs. Bellini, there are certain standards we uphold at this school. We cannot ignore such blatant radicalism."

"I will give the message to Marie's mother. As you know, she is a single working mother and has enough stress. It might be that she will send Marie to a public school. I am sure you will have to explain the loss of tuition to your superiors."

There was silence on the end of the phone. The nun told Angela to have a good day and hung up. That was the last Angela heard about Marie's essay, and Felicia was never informed about the incident.

Angela had taught Marie that she should not pay attention to the opinions of others, and she reinforced this sentiment as much as she could. She also told Marie she should follow her intuition and not involve herself in petty conversation.

"Your Uncle Joe called and said he was coming up from New York City on Sunday. He is looking forward to seeing you," Angela told Marie.

Marie's older brother Robert was named after their father's brother, their uncle Joseph Robert. Because of his effeminate nature and trouble in Catholic school, Joe had moved to Manhattan in 1943 when he was sixteen and would often ride the commuter rail back to Nelsonville for family visits. Angela would say that Joe had a roommate named Dick, but the rest of the family knew that Dick was more than a roommate. The nature of their relationship was never spoken about within the family. Now, at age forty-three, Joe lived with Dick on East 57th and collected modern art.

Marie kissed Angela on the cheek, took the newly hemmed jeans, and left to go horseback riding. "I'll have the dress fitting later today or tomorrow," said Marie.

"You wanted new dresses for school, so don't wait too long. I'll never get them done in time."

Angela smiled. Marie always found a way around things, she mused. That will help her in the future. She could have insisted Marie stay and have her fitting but felt that everyone deserves a good time.

Angela called her friend Lizzy Liamonte.

"We had the FBI police here today looking for my nephew Robert. I'm afraid he's in a lot of trouble."

"I know, Sadie called me."

"You two don't have any secrets, do you?" asked Angela.

"It saves time. I was waiting for your call, and now you don't have to tell me the story."

"I don't know what to do," said Angela. "He may go to jail."

"Don't you know anybody in the military who was close to his father that you could call? Nunzio was in the Reserves and worked with some big wigs at Camp Smith."

"You mean Captain Bonifice?"

"Yeah, weren't he and Nunzio close friends? Didn't Bonifice and his wife have dinner at your house several times? Maybe you can persuade him to help your Robert."

"I don't think he would help a draft dodger."

"Angie, you are persuasive. I am sure you'll think of something. I'm sure he has a skeleton in his closet that you can use to your advantage."

Captain Bonifice had been her nephew Nunzio's closest friend. She would ask for his help, but first she would do some poking into his closet.

"You are good with plans," said Angela. "I should have thought of this myself."

"Just wanted to put a bug in your ear. Good to have a card to play," said Lizzy. "Talk to you later."

Over the years, Angela had recognized her own power to initiate change. The house would not run as smoothly had it not been for her, and she was willing to step up and take charge when necessary.

When Franco was adamantly opposed to renovating the upstairs into a separate apartment, she had convinced him that it was worth the money.

"I'm not spending money on any renovations," Franco said as he waved his arm.

"We can rent it out and make extra money."

"You're making more work for me. I don't want to talk about it, and I don't want strangers living here."

"Maybe one of your nephews and nieces will have a family one day. They can live here. We're alone in this big house and as we grow older, we could use the company."

Franco paused, and Angela saw that it started to make sense to him.

"I'll think about it. Maybe it's not a terrible idea."

Six months later, Angela found Franco and a friend upstairs installing plumbing for a kitchen. Sometimes you must change the physical environment to open to the future, thought Angela. Her unseen friends had told her to prepare the upstairs for the future, so she found a way to dissolve an obstacle. This was the power of persistence in action.

Angela was pinning a pattern for one of her afternoon clients when she heard the doorbell ring. Those FBI men have come back, she worried. She was the only one in the house and she felt trapped. Angela slowly approached the window and peeked out onto the porch, where her friend Sadie stood. She wore large sunglasses and the same clothes she did every day: a faded black skirt, a yellowing white blouse, and an embroidered frayed pocketbook.

"Sadie, come in," said Angela, relieved.

"I came by to finish our conversation," said Sadie. "The doctor says I need to walk more."

"Sadie, your legs are swollen. Come in and put your feet up."

"My heart condition," said Sadie. "It's getting the best of me."

"Are you taking your medication?" asked Angela.

"Sure, when I feel like it. Sometimes my legs are fine. So, your morning wasn't so good?"

"Robert does not want to go to war. I had a conversation with Lizzy this morning, and she gave me an idea."

"Oh yeah, she told me you're blackmailing the captain."

"Do you two live in each other's back pocket? How do you know what we talked about? I am not blackmailing anyone. I am just going to present him with information if needed."

"Sure, call it 'presenting information.' Where is everyone?"

"Felicia is at work, and Frank and Andrea are out. Marie just left for horseback riding. She is going to break a leg someday. You should have seen the clothes she wanted to wear. She looked like a poor person, but I fixed that."

"You dote on her like you did Speranza and her children," said Sadie.

Angela knew this was true but had no regrets.

"Don't be disappointed when she doesn't do what you say or she goes off and does something you don't like," said Sadie.

"Marie will not disappoint me. She has ambition and makes good choices. I can see she will do well. Joe is coming this weekend. I always love seeing him. He has done well for himself. He deserves it."

"You are loyal, Angela."

"I think my great-nieces and nephews will have more of a chance in this country than their parents did. Speranza's children tried, but they made bad choices. I tried to tell them, but they did not listen."

"Joe has done well in the city," said Lizzy. "He attends the theater and has done well working at American Express."

"I suppose, but I wanted him to get an education."

"You can't have everything. Anyway, I just dropped by to say hello. I have to go shopping," said Sadie. "I'll call you later."

Angela was grateful that she had a friend like Sadie, even if she did drink too much and looked like an indigent person.

Angela was frustrated with her inability to have prevented Speranza's children from making mistakes. Even though Joe was doing well, she was unable to convince him to stay in school and go to college. When he was a boy he was a charmer, and the Catholic school nuns did not appreciate his gift of gab. Joe had been bullied, and Angela set it straight. She stood up to the Mother Superior of the school when the nun said Joe was "inappropriate" and a troublemaker. She was so glad she did. In fact, after that, she did not have a problem standing up to the priests in the parish. Once, when a priest said he was disappointed with Franco and Angela's contribution to support the church, they told him that they would have no problem going to the Episcopal church. The priest never complained again.

But that was the first generation born in America. This new generation, her great-nieces and -nephews, was different. American culture was evolving, and the Italian-American community was also in flux. It distressed her at first, because it appeared as if there was no structure. This generation wanted to tear structures down, but how and with what would they replace them? Still, the irreverence intrigued her. It ignited that part of her that never rebelled, because if she had, it would have made her life more difficult than it was.

Angela's great-nieces and -nephews had more opportunity than the previous generation of Italian-Americans. She encouraged them to take advantage of those opportunities. Angela had always had a strategy to accomplish a goal, and if it failed, she tried a different pathway.

The doorbell rang, interrupting her thoughts, and Angela opened the door for her client. Isabella Pullini was a young woman in her early twenties. Her shoulder-length dark hair was elegantly styled, and she wore a navy blue dress with Queen

Anne heels. Her mother had used Angela's services on many occasions, so Isabella wanted Angela to make her a travelling suit. Isabella and her parents were flying to Sicily for a visit. When Angela and Franco travelled to and from Europe, they sailed on a ship. Air travel made the trip to Sicily quick and made short visits to Europe possible. Passengers dressed well to travel on airplanes: hats, gloves, and tailored suits. Isabella wanted to look her best, so she came to Angela.

"I am so glad you have time to make my suit, Mrs. Bellini," said Isabella. She stepped into the hallway where Angela had her sewing machine and mirror. "How long have you been a seamstress?"

"I have sewed since I was a girl," said Angela. "But I came to America fifty-five years ago and began to design clothing." Angela had sewn for many of the wealthy women in town, but the population had changed over the years. In the early 20th century, most of her clients had inherited wealth. The women did not work, and their husbands made a good living. Now, women worked and had disposable income, so Angela's business thrived.

"Mom says you transform people with your designs. She says you bring beauty into the world with what you do."

"What would you want people to think when you put on a garment?" asked Angela.

"I would like an A-line skirt and matching top for the plane trip. I want to look sophisticated on this trip. Mom says there are many young men in Sicily who are interested in marriage."

"Marriage? Have you finished college?" asked Angela.

"I didn't go to college. I work in my father's liquor store. I don't need to go to college."

"I can make a traveling skirt and top that would suggest you are a worldly woman," said Angela. "Wouldn't you like to get an education and do something in the world?"

"I really haven't thought about it," said Isabella. She looked in the mirror and primped her hair.

If someone wanted to get married, who am I to suggest otherwise? thought Angela. She would create a garment that would transform Isabella into an elegant, available young lady.

Angela heard the door unlock. Marie came in with muddy boots and jeans.

"Take those boots off before you walk on my rug. Why couldn't you clean them after you got off the horse? And why are your jeans so filthy?"

"I fell off. We were galloping deep in the forest, and hit a slippery patch." Marie pulled off her boots. Dried mud dropped on the rug, and Marie brushed it under the radiator.

"Isabella, this is my niece, Marie," said Angela. "She never looks like this."

"Sorry to interrupt." She went to climb the stairs.

"When I'm done with Isabella, I'll fit your dress."

"You are so lucky to have your dressmaker living with you," said Isabella. "I would love that. Your aunt is so talented."

"Yeah, she is great," said Marie, smiling.

"I wish I could be as free as you are with your appearance," said Isabella. "My mother would kill me if I went out with jeans and a baggy shirt."

Marie looked at Isabella, thinking that Isabella appeared to be sentenced to a life of dull conservatism without creative thinking.

"Everyone wears jeans," said Marie. "I'm sure you don't dress like that all the time."

"I work in my father's store, so yes, I make sure I look good. You never know who you will meet."

"Meet who?" asked Marie. She knew what she meant but she wanted Isabella to say it.

"A man, of course," said Isabella.

"You're not serious?"

"Marie, go upstairs and take those dirty clothes off right now," said Angela.

Angela knew Marie's tactics in spinning the conversation so she could put forth her ideas. Marie was the poster child for

1960s counterculture. But Angela wanted to do Isabella's fitting, not hear a lecture on why conservatism was dead.

"Ok, I'm going. It's been really weird, Isabella."

"Isabella, take this in my bedroom and try it on," said Angela.

As Isabella waked away, Angela waved Marie to go upstairs as if she was chasing away a fly.

"So annoying," mumbled Marie.

"What did you say?" asked Angela.

"Not a thing," said Marie, running up the stairs.

Angela smiled. In her heart she was glad that Marie had a rebellious streak.

Marie bounded down the stairs for her fitting.

"This print will suit you," said Angela. She held up a small, flowered print dress with sleeves that billowed at the wrist. It was fitted at the waist, and the hem was just below the knee.

"I love the sleeves," said Marie. "But let's make it a mini."

"That's too short for school."

"It's not for school. It's a fun dress."

"I'll ask your mother when she comes home."

"She doesn't care about my hem."

"Try it on please," said Angela. "I wish you would try to get along with your mother. She works so hard."

"We get along as long as she doesn't tell me what to do."

For Marie, the hustle and bustle in the house on Morning Glory Avenue made it possible for her to be a fly on the wall and observe. Her friends interpreted this as shy passivity, but it was strategy; Marie had no desire to be criticized for her choices. Quiet by nature, she kept a low profile and made detachment an art.

"You have the reputation of being a miracle worker with clothes," said Marie. "Every time I wear one of your dresses, my friends comment that I look different. Your work is so beautiful."

"That is what I do. I transform through what I create."

"You transform human beings," Marie said, "and that is a miracle worker."

"Choose work that transfigures people for good. Listen to your intuition."

"You keep saying that, but how do I know I'm using my intuition? You talk to people who aren't here. Tell me about that."

Angela felt her spiritual beliefs that were outside of church doctrine were not to be revealed or discussed. To Angela, her connection to her unseen friends was deep alchemy and should be practiced privately, but for Marie she made an exception.

"When I was young, my life needed help from the other side. Because of that need, I have communicated with unseen beings, or people, and they have never failed me."

"Is that your intuition?"

"I think it is connected, but I'm not certain. I think you should follow your inner insights and see where that leads you."

"You mean visions?" asked Marie, turning to look at Angela. Their conversations never lacked insight and inspiration. Their deep connection was obvious.

"Or a strong feeling, like a nudge."

"You know, when I was a little girl I remember jumping up and down on my bed with my eyes closed and sensing different beings and feeling uplifted to a higher space, but as soon as I opened my eyes and stopped jumping, I was in my room. I thought I had left the room, but I think I left my body." Marie thought of that experience from time to time, it was as if she had taken a brief vacation from her present life.

"It could have been your imagination," said Angela. "You always had a great imagination." It was clear to Angela that Marie's experience was beyond imagery or vision and that she was making a connection to other spaces, but she felt that was a conversation for another time.

Marie stepped up on the platform in front of the full-length mirror. Angela had fitted two generations of family before Marie. They had all stood in front of the same mirror, and every time the mirror seemed to spark a universal conversation. The pettiness of everyday life melted away, and a space opened to talk about subjects that otherwise would not be discussed.

Angela remembered cautioning Marie about staring into the mirror when she was a child.   Marie usually found it difficult to stay still during a fitting, but when she was nine years old and Angela was busy marking the hem on her dress, Marie remained still and seemed to tilt toward the mirror. Angela looked up and saw Marie transfixed, eyes wide open, staring into the mirror.

"Marie," Angela had said to the girl, shaking her. "Look away from that mirror. How many times have I told you not to stare into the mirror?"

It was obvious Marie was drawn to the looking glass and the world inside, but she was too young at that time for the experiences waiting in the mirror's environment, so Angela discouraged it.   From then on, Angela had Marie face away from the mirror when she did alterations or fitted her for a garment.

When Angela had her own experience with the full-length mirror at the convent, she was older and had a relationship with her unseen friends. Convent life was the perfect ambiance to develop a connection with the unseen world. The interior was designed for a contemplative, prayerful life even though it was part of Palazzo Butera and the surroundings were lush. The nuns stressed focus and a connection to the divine. Life in America had sped up, and it was easy to become distracted and lose all contact with the unseen world.

"Who was that girl you were fitting?"

"She is the daughter of Mrs. Pullini. You remember her."

"Isn't she the one who lost her son in the Second World War?"

"Yes, that's right. Then she was blessed with Isabella later in life."

Angela gazed at Marie's reflection. Speranza, Marie's grandmother, had stood here as Angela fitted her for her wedding dress. That was over thirty years ago, but memories were energy that could be ignited with a wisp of a thought. The past and present could mesh with a memory that came crashing into one's mind.

"There were Pullinis who lived on the Lower East Side where your uncle and I lived when we first came here. I wonder if they are related," thought Angela out loud.

"You lived on the Lower East Side when you came to New York City?"

"We lived on Goerck Street. I had never experienced such tight quarters. The convent had been large and spacious with corridors that were so long they seemed to extend into the next town."

"Was it a tenement?"

"Yes, we were there for a few months until our home was ready in Nelsonville. I met your grandmother in that tenement, and I felt I had found my purpose; to take care of Speranza."

On the first night in the tenement on Goerck Street, Angela had dreamed that her unseen friends were leading her down a path. There were always two of them, and they appeared to her differently each time. In this dream, they were two Botticelli-like women with wavy shoulder-length hair and round eyes. They gently escorted her past opulent trees with deep green oval-shaped leaves until they came to a meadow where the foliage turned to gold and yellow, and Black-eyed Susans peppered the landscape. The women gestured Angela forward. She would take the rest of the journey on her own. Angela looked back at her unseen friends and they both nodded, and she waved. They would be close by, but she would have to walk her new path alone.

Angela awoke early that next morning comforted that her unseen friends had made the journey with her, as it increased her confidence to face the new world. The shared apartment was still asleep as she walked to the kitchen to make a pot of coffee. This was her home now, and she wanted to make a good impression; she wanted to be helpful.

Maybe the benevolence of the universe and her connection to her unseen friends saved her from the earthquake. Why she deserved such favor she did not know, but since God had been so generous in sparing her life, she felt she needed to share her good fortune with everyone in her orbit.

"You're my sister now," said the young Speranza as she entered the kitchen. Her long braids were frayed at the ends, and she had holes in her nightgown.

"I will sew the holes in your nightgown today."

"That would be nice of you. My brother loves you, so I love you."

Angela soon had forgotten about her dream and focused on the care of her new sister-in-law.

When the house renovations were finished in Nelsonville, Angela, Franco, Franco's mother and Speranza moved in. The house had three bedrooms with a small dining room, living room, and kitchen. It was a dwelling with a large backyard and plenty of room to extend the house. Angela felt she was looking at her new life from a precipice with innumerable opportunities below her. She was certain she had made the right choice in leaving Sicily.

"You were brave," said Marie. "Why did you marry Uncle Franco and come to America? You didn't know what you were in for." Marie loved hearing this story about Angela's fortitude.

"What choice did I have? I could have stayed at the convent where it was safe and become a nun. But after meeting your uncle, I knew that he chose me for a reason."

"I guess you'd heard stories about America," said Marie. "Maybe you thought everyone was rich."

"No, but I was sure that my life would be freer. That is the key: freedom."

Angela surprised herself with her response. She had never thought about freedom as a concept. She developed her business, became successful, and helped raise a new generation of Americans, all by choice. Maybe that is what freedom is, thought Angela, the ability to contribute your talents and ideas to anyone able to accept them. Freedom was not just about the ability to travel and live where you wanted. It was about controlling your destiny and not feeling like you're fated. One had to take control and write one's own story.

"I agree with you," said Marie. "I just have to figure out how I'm going to be free in the future."

"That is a good goal," said Angela. "You should think about a time when you were a child that made you feel happy. That took you away."

"That's easy! It was when you took me to St. Mary's Episcopal School, and I sat by the pond and communicated with the tadpoles. That took me away."

Marie remembered watching the tadpoles that lived in the pond, picking them up and placing them on lily pads. She felt she was invited into their home, and a blanket of peace surrounded her. She felt at home then, and she was able to reach into the tadpoles' reality and see the gifts they showered on the natural world. She loved being accepted into their environment. It made sense to her.

"Tadpoles represent a desire for adventure. I think that suits you."

"I would love to have many adventures like the one you had when you came to America."

"I hope you get everything you wish for."

"You've had a lot of people stand in front of this mirror," said Marie.

"You will probably be the last generation I'll sew for. I am glad it ends with you."

"Why?"

"Because you are the generation that is the furthest away from life in Sicily, so you will be the freest to choose your destiny."

"You mean after I graduate high school, you won't sew anymore?"

"I will sew for you and your sister for as long as I can, and then I will give it up."

Angela accepted her aging body and realized she had a certain amount of time left. Her hair was completely gray, but she still had a straight posture and smooth skin with very few lines. She was in her seventies, and she could still walk up the steep hill to St. Mary's Convent where she occasionally sewed for the nuns. Angela's posture was one of the most noticeable physical characteristics that attracted Franco when he visited the convent in Sicily. It suggested to him that this was someone who could stand up to the challenges in life. And he was right. Angela had sailed through every storm with her posture intact. A strong spine suggested a strong foundation.

She wanted to leave her story to someone. Marie was the perfect person to begin sharing more of her experiences with, not only as being an immigrant woman in America, but as someone with a connection with the unseen world. With every tragedy in her life, she turned to her connection with the concealed world. After a serious illness that prevented her from having children, her disembodied friends told her that one day, she would have a family. She now had her four great-nieces and -nephews living upstairs whom she now influenced, and she had helped to raise Speranza's three children. Sometimes you just had to wait for things to happen.

"At the convent, there was only one full-length mirror and that was near the Mother Superior's office. Vanity was considered a sin, so we only had small mirrors to make sure our hair was in place."

Angela pinned the hem on Marie's dress below her knees.

"Can you make the hem above my knees? This is the 1960s, not the 1860s."

Marie yawned and turned to look at the hall clock as Angela shortened the hem.

"But there was an unspoken reason that the girls were cautioned against full length mirrors. There were whispers, especially from the nuns, that mirrors were doorways to other places and that souls could be trapped in the dimension of the looking glass."

Marie had never heard that mirrors were portals. This was new.

"What do you mean? People were stuck in the mirrors?"

"I think the mirror can catch people's energy, and they feel drained," said Angela.

"Really? You mean I could get trapped?"

"We don't stare into it for any length of time, so we don't have to worry. But if you were to stare, things might start to appear. When I am done with sewing, I will take it into the yard and smash it."

"I think I see into other spaces," said Marie. "I have a gut feeling about things."

"And that is a good thing. You should also daydream, because that opens more of what you can see. Your Uncle Joe was the same. He could see, but he never developed it."

Angela recalled an incident at the convent with the only full-length mirror permitted by the Mother Superior. Angela had stood in front of the mirror in her wedding dress to see if any more alterations were needed. As Angela gazed into the looking glass, she descended deeply into its environment and she saw shapes appearing, then disappearing. Angela touched the glass and energy rippled out like water, but she was afraid to go any further. She shared her experience with one of the girls, and the next day the girl decided to have her own experience with the mirror. She was found that evening lying unconscious in front of the mirror. When the girl woke, she said she had seen her dead mother and sister attempting to ascend into heaven, but they were pulled down by evil creatures dressed in black.

Angela thought that maybe if she had peered long and hard enough into the looking glass, she would have found her parents and siblings. Angela longed to see her family again. Maybe she would have, if she had conquered her fear.

"Probably because it is kind of wild to think about," Marie said.

"You know, when I left Sicily, I worried that my connection to my inside voices would leave. My voices said that time and place would not affect our communication."

"Do you talk to them every day? Are they listening to us now?"

"I don't know, but I can talk to them whenever I want, even late at night."

"Were they once alive?"

"Yes, I think so; that's why their advice is so valuable."

Marie experienced a connection to home within herself when her aunt talked about the occult world. Her own existence seemed validated, and it strengthened her sense of self. She knew Angela loved the Blessed Mother and believed that Mary had saved her life when she was ill years ago. She had never shared her aunt's story with any of her friends; she kept it close to her heart. She had the sense that her aunt's stories would prove to be useful someday, but she was cautious about sharing them. But Marie was ready to explore and see what she could experience. Many people used drugs to attain such levels of awareness—all her aunt did was believe and connect.

While Angela focused on reshaping a dart on the dress and feeling she was at the precipice of a new life, Marie decided to stare as hard as she could into her reflection to see if she could access this other world. At first, she focused on looking into her eyes. She turned her head to the side while keeping her gaze on the mirror and placed her fingertips on the glass, attempting to reach into the other dimension. Suddenly she began to see beyond her eyes into a small dark space that expanded as she focused. As she investigated the glass, the reflection of the back wall faded, and the glass began to ripple under her fingertips. Marie felt a vibration under her fingers, the sensation soothing but ominous. She sensed the mirror was beckoning her, and she felt if she could let go of her traditional views of reality, she could fall through. She lifted her foot and wondered if she should take that step forward.

She was drawn to travel the planet but also to other densities. To Marie it was not extraordinary—it was her birthright. Once she accessed the mirror's interior, a white emptiness surrounded her, and it felt like she had entered a blank canvas waiting for her intention to paint her vision. In that space, Marie walked around and wondered what she should create. A clear vision was missing, so the area remained white and anticipatory, waiting for Marie to begin.

"Is anybody here?" called Marie in her mind. She felt a coolness caress her skin and a slight movement under her feet.

A small figure emerged from the distance and waved her forward.

"Hello," said Marie as she waved.

The figure hesitated to come forward, so Marie walked toward it. As Marie drew closer, she saw that it was a young woman dressed in 1920s vintage garb.

"Do I know you?" asked Marie.

The woman stared at her as if waiting for Marie to recognize her.

"Tell me who you are and why you're here," Marie said.

As Marie looked closer, she recognized her grandmother Speranza's features: the strong nose, long neck, and soft brown eyes she'd seen in family photos.

"Speranza, right?"

The woman smiled and radiated a warm yellow light toward Marie. She heard her grandmother talking, but her lips did not move. She somehow threw Marie her thoughts.

"I was like you," said Speranza. "Use your talents. Do not waste them. Listen to Aunt Angela. I should have."

Marie felt a conflict between her personal ambitions and her natural talents. No one would understand or consider her capabilities valid. How could she use her talent for listening and problem-solving through her intuition, and pick a college major that would develop them? She doubted that she could major in mirror gazing.

"I won't be accepted by people," said Marie. "I would like to fit in."

She shared her experiences once with some girlfriends, but it did not seem to make her popular in high school.

"You will become more popular if you become a cheerleader," said one of her friends. "You need to try out."

"But I don't know anything about sports, and I don't know the players," Marie had said. "Why would I cheer for people I don't know?"

"Nobody really knows them. It's how you become part of the important crowd. There's nothing else to do in this town."

"You could develop your intuition," said Marie. "You could spend the day in New York City and explore. Those are things to do."

"What do you mean develop your intuition? What is that? My parents say New York City is dangerous and dirty. We never go there. Tryouts are this afternoon. I'll put you on the list. Say you'll come."

Her friend turned and walked away before Marie could respond, holding her books to the chest. Marie thought maybe she should try out. If she were a cheerleader, maybe she would enjoy high school more and the time would go faster. She did not like to cheer and could care less about winning, but she could feign interest. She wasn't surprised when she didn't make the team.

"I thought that once," Speranza replied. "I told myself that people would not listen to me, but I was wrong—some will. You must find them. There will be those who ridicule, but keep in mind those are the ones who lack vision."

Speranza faded, and Marie turned to leave the white space when a dark image appeared in front of her. It was a ragged woman with moth-eaten clothes and black, deep-set eyes. Marie stepped back and then suddenly found herself standing in front of the mirror.

She kissed and hugged Angela.

"I just saw grandma in the mirror. I just saw her!"

"I had hoped you would not do that. You need to be careful. You never know what is in there."

"I'm not sure what it all means," said Marie. "Is it real?"

"You know it is, but you don't need to worry about that now. When you go to college there is no need to talk about seeing things. You will just create problems for yourself."

"I want to travel first, before I do anything."

"That is what your Uncle Joe said, and he never went to college. Do not forget he will be here this weekend. And another thing, do not tell your mother."

"About what?"

"Your experiences and wanting to travel before college. You will start a war."

They both knew that Felicia was steeped in the material world and did not consider the possibility of life beyond the physical. In her view, any spiritual needs one had should be dictated by the Catholic Church. The teachings of the church were ordered and clear. She sensed that Marie had a strong ethereal side and felt it was her obligation to bring Marie back to earth.

"Don't you want to know what grandma said?"

"I know she wants you to follow your way, but remember you live in this world. You do not want to get them mixed up."

"You always talk about unseen beings."

"With you, and because I am old and have lived my life. You need to be more cautious because your life is just beginning, and people may ridicule you and that may make you isolated and angry. You don't have time for that. You, your sister, and brothers are on the road to success in this country. You need to do that."

"What about my intuitive ability?"

Finishing making the dress, Angela said, "You will need to be mindful about who you share it with. You need to live between the worlds."

"How do you do that?"

"You speak with the unseen world and you do it in private and then take what you learned into your life. People will notice that you have wisdom. Now let's talk about what to make for Uncle Joe's visit this coming Sunday."

Marie loved and looked forward to visits with Joe. He and Dick had travelled the globe, and she loved hearing stories about where they had been and the people they met. Joe influenced her love of New York City and adventure from an early age. When she was seven years old, Joe had taken Marie's entire family on a tour of Manhattan. She remembered eating at Horn and Hardart across from Grand Central Station, having lunch in Chinatown, and dinner at a Swedish smorgasbord. The rest of the day was seeing all the sights: The Empire State

Building, The Statue of Liberty, Little Italy, and Greenwich Village.

On that day, Marie developed a love of new places and connected with the vibrant energy of the city, becoming a "city person" from that day forward. Now at the age of sixteen, her favorite pastime was skipping school and exploring New York. Whenever she stepped off the train in Grand Central, she felt completely free.

Angela busily prepared a special Sunday dinner and waited for Joe to arrive. Felicia was setting the dining room table, and the household was filled with chatter. Felicia was petite with bright, dark eyes and wavy hair; a vivacious, impeccably dressed woman who enjoyed parties and lively gatherings.

When they had guests, Angela and Felicia cooked an elaborate meal where everyone would sit at the table all afternoon. Marie's oldest brother, Frank, came up the porch stairs.

"Where is everyone?" asked Frank. He had long black hair, a trimmed beard, and wore a t-shirt and jeans. He looked the part of the New York University engineering student with a deferment from the Vietnam War because he was in college. Felicia intended to educate all her children but demanded that they choose a practical major.

"Inside cooking," said Marie. "Where do you think?"

"Another marathon meal, huh?" commented Frank.

"Yeah, they've made two cakes for dessert. By the time lunch, is done it will be time for dinner. I think Aunt Angela has invited a few of her friends. Sadie and Lizzy are coming—it should be a free-for-all."

Lizzy and Sadie made Joe laugh, and the more he laughed the more outrageous the conversation became. It was entertainment at its best, and it was free for those who were invited.

Marie could hear her mother's purposeful step in the vestibule. Felicia started to talk before she opened the screen door.

"What are you two doing?" asked Felicia.

"Nothing," said Marie.

"Get dressed for lunch. I have to pick your uncle up at the station in a few minutes."

"I'm dressed," said Frank.

"I can wear my jeans," said Marie. "What difference does it make?"

"Your uncle will probably be in a suit, so put on something else. I don't know why you give me so much trouble. Just put on something else."

"Let's just wait and see if Uncle Joe approves. I won't change until he tells me to." Uncle Joe won't care what I have on and my mother knows it, thought Marie.

"Felicia," called Angela, "help me turn over the chicken before it burns."

"Get changed now," said Felicia.

Proper dress for Sunday dinner was a household tradition, but over the years had become lax. In past decades, all the women wore dresses and men wore suits. Now such a dress code seemed silly in the turbulent 1960s.

Marie went inside to look in the full-length mirror to see how her jeans and peasant top looked. Hippy chic and perfect, she thought. There was bohemian in her uncle, so he would not mind her attire. She paused to look deeper into the mirror but heard her mother's car pull up.

The screen door opened, and Joe and Felicia sauntered in.

"Joe, it's so good to see you," said Angela. She embraced and kissed him on both cheeks.

"How are you, Aunt Angela?" asked Joe. "You're looking as elegant as ever. You never change."

Joe was dressed in a silk Armani suit complete with gold cufflinks. A diamond pinky ring sparkled on his finger as the sun streamed in through the stained-glass window and reflected its light on the diamond. The silk suit seemed to glow in the sunlight, creating an aura around him.

Angela stood back and looked at her nephew. It didn't seem that long ago that she had stood at the Nelsonville train station and seen sixteen-year-old Joe off to his new life in New

York City. She remembered crying and holding on to her Franco. Here it was almost thirty years later, and Joe had made himself a success working at the American Express travel office selling exotic vacations to the rich. Angela felt that she had had a hand in developing his drive and success as Joe's mother, Speranza, had died when Joe was a young boy and his father, needing a new wife, went back to Sicily and married his niece. This was something Angela would never forgive.

"Marie, love the outfit," said Joe.

"Aunt Angela wanted me to change," said Marie. "I'm glad you like it."

"It's very hippy chic," said Joe.

"That's exactly what I said," said Marie.

Joe winked at Marie. He gets me, she thought, and she looked at her mother with a self-satisfied smile.

"Never mind that, let's go to the table," said Felicia. She disliked fuss being made over her children. She feared that if they received too much praise and approval, they would not try hard enough to succeed. Angela provided the praise, and Felicia the criticism.

"What about Sadie and Lizzy?" asked Marie.

Marie's younger sister, Andrea, rushed in dripping wet.

"Have you been jumping into other people's pools again?" asked Felicia. "Go upstairs and dry off and put on some decent clothes."

"She must be a handful," said Joe.

"I'm sorry, Joe, she's very stubborn," said Felicia.

When Angela was raising Joe and his siblings, children did not talk back, and discussion was saved for the dining room table. There was an order to behavior and speech. It pleased Angela that her nieces were bold and thought for themselves, even if she complained about it.

Everyone went into the dining room and took their seats.

"Oh, homemade bread," said Joe, "it's just scrumptious. Where are the other guests?"

On cue, the doorbell rang.

"I'll get it," called Andrea.

Loud laughter radiated from the hallway into the dining room.

"They're here," called Andrea, on her way upstairs to change.

"Hello, ladies," said Joe. He lit a Gauloise cigarette and took a long drag. "It's good to see you."

"Good to see you, Joe," said Lizzy. "It's been a while."

"I know," said Joe. "So, anyone find a new husband? I know you ladies are flying solo. Attractive women like yourselves should have no problem."

"I'll sit next to you, Sadie," said Andrea, wearing dry clothes.

"Why not? You seem like a good person to sit next to," said Sadie. "Joe, you devil, you know I'm too old."

"Nonsense, you still have life in you," said Joe. He flicked his ashes in the glass ashtray.

Angela placed the antipasto on the table.

"Don't you think Sadie should marry again, Aunt Angela?" asked Joe.

Everyone laughed, including Sadie. Angela loved the lightness of the conversation. After a lifetime of taking care of an invalid husband and three generations of family, she was glad to have the levity.

"You're a good sport, Sadie," said Angela. "Everyone, eat the antipasto."

"I'd be a better sport if you poured me some wine," said Sadie.

"Where is Robert?" Joe whispered in Marie's ear.

"Don't ask," said Marie.

"Ooh, sounds intriguing."

Angela poured everyone a glass of red wine.

"To peace," said Angela. She lifted her glass and hoped the war would come to an end before they found Robert.

"I agree, Aunt Angela," said Joe. "Thank God I'm too old to fight. I'm just useless when it comes to marching, and the guns are too heavy for my delicate physique."

Lizzy and Sadie laughed.

"There is nothing wrong with being delicate," said Angela. "I always tell Marie to marry someone delicate, someone simpatico, someone who is not afraid of change."

Angela had identified as an orphan and earthquake survivor since she immigrated, but she was more than that now. In a sense she helped mold this country into what it was and what it was becoming. The consensus was that nothing could hold you back in America if you were determined to succeed, and if you were held back it was because you did not see the abundance of opportunity available.

"Felicia, how about a New York shopping trip?" Joe asked. "It's on me. I know that Dick would love to spend time with you." Joe lifted his pinky finger and sipped his wine.

"I don't need anything," said Felicia. "But I would love to come down and have a visit."

Marie's mother and uncle had had a deep connection ever since her father first introduced Felicia to Joe in New York in the early 1940s. They both loved to dance and gossip about family, and she made sure Joe was invited to all the family gatherings. He praised her on how well she was raising the children, and she basked in that praise. Regardless of whether she had help, she was still a widowed single mother who struggled to have a career and make sure the children were cared for as best she could.

"Marie and Andrea, would you two care to come?" asked Joe.

"I'll go," said Marie.

"Don't know," said Andrea. "It depends on what my friends are doing."

Angela was glad that Joe shared some of his life with his family. She had favored him as a child, while Franco had connected more with Nunzio. Angela attempted to impart her heritage's culture to Joe. He expressed interest in cooking, opera and fashion. She could see that Joe was carrying on their tradition of dressing well. Not in the same way, but she could see that he maintained a sense of Italian culture.

"You ladies have not said a word about my suit," said Joe. He took off his jacket and held it up.

"That's a beautiful suit," Lizzy said, winking at him.

"Yeah," said Sadie. "I'd marry you myself if you were my age. You're fairly good eye candy."

Angela lit the taper candles in the center of the table, standing like sentries next to the fresh cut flowers. Silver flatware graced the sides of the china that Franco had bought when they first married, and the pressed white linen tablecloth was fine enough to create a garment.

Angela and Felicia brought out platters of chicken, pasta, and eggplant parmesan. The meal extended into the late afternoon. Angela sat at the head of the table and passed the platters around the table. The aroma of each dish permeated the dining room; garlic, parmesan cheese, and red sauce created a feast for the senses.

"Tell me what everyone is doing," said Joe, cutting a piece of chicken.

"I have great professors in mechanical technology and drafting," said Frank. "I'm looking forward to landing a job in Manhattan."

"At least you got out of the draft," said Joe. "I always like to see a man in uniform, but I don't like the fighting."

"I agree with you," said Marie.

"What about you, Andrea? What do you think?"

"I don't care. I don't think about it, except the police are after Robert and I miss him."

"Let's not talk about the war and enjoy our meal," said Angela.

"Why not?" asked Frank. "We're all against it."

"They're all killing each other over there," said Felicia. "I think they need to pull out so my son can come home."

"There are a lot of protests," said Marie. "They will have to pull out eventually. Who wants to fight this war?"

"I sure don't," said Frank. "I'm glad I'm in college."

"But once you graduate, you could be drafted," said Joe. "You need to think ahead. I don't blame Robert for not wanting to go into the army."

"No more talk about the war," said Felicia. Silence fell over the dining room like a wet blanket, as everyone knew that when Felicia spoke, it was best not to challenge her. It was times like these that she felt most alone. She felt she had no one to assist her when she was up against a force like the government.

"So, Joe, how is your job at American Express going?" asked Sadie, sipping her wine.

"I am no longer working. Dick has produced a few successful B movies, and I am now a free man."

"Here's to you," said Sadie as she lifted her wine glass.

"What films?" asked Marie.

"Horror films," said Joe. "He produced *Corridors of Blood* and *The Haunted Strangler.*"

"That is wonderful news, Joe," Angela said. "How will you spend your time?"

"I have plenty to do at home. I am going to redecorate our apartment and Dick's office."

A cacophony of voices filled the air as everyone spoke simultaneously.

Joe smiled, sat back and pushed his plate away. "I am stuffed. This was delicious—as good as any restaurant in New York."

"It's time for dessert," said Angela. "Italian cheesecake and lemon meringue pie."

"Not for me, said Joe. "I have to watch my figure. I'll take a slice home."

"Do you remember when we made cannoli when you were a kid?" asked Angela.

"I do, Angela, and those are my best memories. You were good to me, and I appreciate it every day. I felt loved."

"Pass the wine," said Sadie.

"It's been lovely dining with you, family." Joe glanced at his gold watch. "My train leaves in a half hour."

Marie and Angela began to clear the table.

"I'll take you to the station. Lizzy and Sadie, I can take you home too."

"Oh, Felicia, you are a gem," said Lizzy. "I can't walk as fast as I used to."

Angela felt grateful for a day that included laughter and lively conversation; it brightened the week ahead.

"I will help finish the dishes," said the returning Felicia as she closed the side door.

"I think we can get Captain Bonifice to help get Robert home," Angela offered.

"I know," said Felicia. "Sadie told me what you were thinking."

"That woman. She never keeps quiet. Let's invite him for dinner. I want to get this over with."

Angela and Felicia finished putting the dishes away in silence.

"You should not worry so much about the kids. They're my children, so they're my responsibility."

"They are my concern too," said Angela. "I want to help."

"You don't help by codling them. They need to grow up."

"Listen, I was all alone in the world at the convent. I grew up without parents. So, what you call codling I call love and concern. They're my nephew's children, and my joy was to help raise them."

"Yes, but I make the decisions about discipline."

"You do, but I am there when those decisions don't work."

Felicia knew that Angela's input and help had been invaluable. Her children grew up in a supportive and stable environment, partly due to Angela.

"Let's talk about planning this dinner tomorrow. I'm tired and need to get some sleep," said Felicia.

"See you tomorrow. Thank you."

A ngela sat in Franco's smoking chair in the dining room. She felt an opening sensation at the crown of her head and knew her unseen friends wanted to communicate. She could hear them most often when she was tired and ready to rest. Sometimes they worked in images, but tonight they presented a distant memory. When she was young, before the 1908 earthquake, she remembered a conversation with her parents.

"Mario, I don't understand why they want you out of the guild," Angela's mother, Rosa, had said. "I would consult the head of the guild and see if he can help. They cannot just throw you out without an inquiry."

Mario travelled to many exotic countries buying and selling silk. He loved his job, and it supported his family, but the poor who made the silk were paid little.

"I will continue to do business, but not in the way they want," said Mario.

"You'll just make more trouble for yourself," said Rosa. Mario paid workers extra out of his wages when he picked up the silk. The guild was against this, even though there was not a law stipulating differently.

Angela breathed deeply and brought herself back to the present, confused about what she had been shown. It felt random to Angela, but sometimes it took months to understand why she was shown an image or conversation. She understood how that conversation molded her, and to this day she never hesitated to help someone less fortunate. Angela looked around the dining room and smiled.

She had survived all the challenges in her seventy-three years, but there was still work to be done with the new generation. The oppression of women who pursued financial independence through business was less obvious in America than Sicily, but it was there, lurking in the background like a silent, indiscernible shadow. This challenge did not come from the government or from the aristocracy but from within the Italian-American community.

When Angela first started to sew for private clients, her friends discouraged her.

"Why not work in a factory where they make clothes? You would have a steady income. If you work on your own, people may not come."

"I agree," had said Ramina Galucci. Her husband was a respected tailor in town, and she did not want the competition.

Even though Angela primarily designed women's clothes, she had also made men's suits and shirts. In the Italian-American community, the possibility of Angela becoming successful on her own was beyond their realm of possibility. Her unseen friends encouraged her to persevere, and she had. She had her doubts at first, but she had accomplished her goal.

Angela rested her head against the back of her husband's chair and closed her eyes, content. It had been a long day. Joe was successful, and she had a business because she did not give up.

"Aunt Angela, can I have a piece of cake?" asked Marie. "Oh, I'm sorry, were you asleep?"

"No, I was resting my eyes. Come in the kitchen, I'll have a piece too."

"Uncle Joe looked good," said Marie. She sat at the kitchen table as Angela cut two pieces of cheesecake.

"Yes, your uncle has done well, and you will too," said Angela.

"I don't think I'll ever be able to afford an Armani suit."

"Women don't wear suits," said Angela. "Doing well in life does not mean you can buy an Armani suit. It is just a representation of good quality. Now eat your cake."

"Doing well in life means you can afford an Armani suit," said Marie, "but choose not to because you live a quality life. Like you, Aunt Angela."

Chapter 2
THE OTHER HALF

Felicia and Marie walked through Grand Central Station on their way to Joe's apartment on East 57th Street. Marie wore a long-sleeved royal blue and white one-piece culotte garment created by Angela. It was a sunny September Saturday with a hint of fall in the air. Autumn in New York was refreshing after a hot steamy summer. The entire city took on a rejuvenated feel as people sauntered through green areas and lifted their faces to the sun to take in rays of renewal.

"Can we go to a museum?" asked Marie.

"I don't think we want to spend today in a museum. It's such a beautiful day."

Marie was accustomed to the subject of her mother' and uncle's conversation. They consistently engaged in family gossip whenever they met. They would talk about Marie's step-grandmother and grandfather, aunts and uncles, and any cousins who were misbehaving. All family members were gossip fodder; no one was spared from their criticism and judgment. If Marie were lucky, she would be able to steer the conversation in a more favorable direction.

The doorman swung the door open for Marie and her mother. He dialed the phone in the lobby.

"Sir, your sister-in-law and niece are here."

The doorman wore a bright red full-length coat with brass buttons and a matching red hat. Marie thought his outfit looked like something you would find in a vintage shop in Greenwich Village. Most of the buildings in the mid to upper East Side had doormen and concierges.

Joe was waiting for them with his apartment door open as they exited the elevator.

"Hello, my darlings, it's so good to see you," said Joe.

The small apartment's walls were covered with modern and contemporary art. A large, generous couch with plush chairs surrounded a glass coffee table. Wine and martini glasses hung over the bar.

"I have made some coffee. Care for a cup?"

"Yes, that would be fine," said Felicia.

"Sure," said Marie.

"Marie, that is a fabulous outfit—very young and fun."

"Aunt Angela made it for me," said Marie. It seemed to Marie that Angela attended get-togethers through her creations.

"I have a shirt she made me years ago," said Joe. "I can't bring myself to throw it out."

They started to talk about Joe's sister, Alicia.

"I don't know what she's going to do if she gains any more weight," said Joe. "She won't get a man that way." He took a sip of his coffee. "Sometimes she asks Dick and me for money."

"Nunzio gave her money one time, but she never paid us back," said Felicia. "I'm still waiting for it."

Marie used this window of opportunity. "Would you mind if I went out and walked around the neighborhood? I'm doing a sociology project for school about the development of the East Side of New York. The library isn't far."

"Be back in an hour for lunch," said Felicia.

"She could meet us at the restaurant," said Joe.

"That's a great idea," said Marie.

"No, it's not. Be back here in an hour. Understand?"

"Better listen to mama," said Joe. He lifted his cup in a toast.

Marie made a right onto 57th Street, walked to 5th Avenue and then headed toward 42nd Street. She had walked New York streets since she was seven years old, and the experience was consistently the same: she felt confident and light. Marie planned to apply to colleges in Manhattan for an early acceptance. It didn't matter what college and she wasn't sure of her major, but she was adamant about living in the city. She made a right onto 42nd Street and entered Bryant Park. It was filled with New Yorkers and tourists taking pictures. Marie sat on a bench and wondered how she could make the next two years in high school bearable. She would have to spend as much time as she could in Manhattan, and once she got accepted into college, she would spend little time in class.

Marie felt the warmth of the sun on her head. She lifted her face and allowed the rays to permeate her skin. The temperature was rising, and the diaphanous material on her sleeves stuck to her arms. She looked at the shiny gold buttons on her cuffs. The buttonholes were meticulously made by hand. Angela's garments echoed her delicate sensibility and strength.

She wondered how long it would take for Felicia and Joe to go through every member of the family and discuss their faults and put their lives under the microscope of criticism. They both enjoyed gossip, and Felicia's mood usually lightened after they sufficiently disapproved of everyone in the family. On this glorious day with the sun shining down, Marie got to take in Manhattan on her own terms.

Marie glanced at her watch. If there was anything Felicia hated it was tardiness, believing that if you wanted to be successful in life, you had to be on time—no exceptions. Marie observed people as they sauntered by. People holding maps pointed and looked up at the famous library. They were fleeting figures that spoke Italian, French, and Spanish. She looked up at the sun, and in her mind's eye she saw shadows of people who once occupied the same space. These images were superimposed over the present day, but felt like they were from another century: men in black hats, high collars, and suits. The women wore long dresses and elaborate hats. A feeling of expansiveness pervaded Marie's body as if a spotlight were flipped on, lighting up the cells of her body. She looked at her watch and decided to go in the library.

She browsed the exhibits that displayed the history of the library. As she stood in front of an old map of New York, a woman and her college-aged son stood beside her.

"Now I've told you, keep your nose in your studies at Columbia. Your father and I are spending a lot of money on your education. If you want to get into Columbia Law School when you graduate, you will need to do well as an undergrad."

Marie looked at the young man. He wore a loose jacket over a t-shirt and jeans. He smiled sheepishly at Marie and shrugged his shoulders.

"It sounds familiar," said Marie.

The mother and son turned to leave the library. The young man looked back at Marie with a grin that lifted her spirit. His warm brown eyes glistened as the sun streamed in from the library windows. It was comforting to Marie that someone had the same mother she had, just different bodies.

On her way back to Joe's apartment, she stopped at a street vendor and bought a blue headband that matched her outfit. It was a nice touch, she thought.

"This is a lovely place," said Felicia. "I think I'll have a highball."

"Ooh, that sounds good, except I'll have a Martini," said Joe. He put his cigarette in a holder and lit up.

"I'd like a sherry," said Marie.

"You'll have a Coke," said Felicia.

"Waiter," said Joe, "the young lady will have a Coke."

Her uncle had deferred to her mother ever since Marie could remember, fearing her wrath. Felicia was the only person Joe never criticized.

"Where did you get the headband?" asked Felicia.

"I bought it from a street vendor. It matches my outfit."

"Where did you get the money?"

"Aunt Angela gave me money to spend."

Felicia did not like Angela giving her children money. She believed that Angela spoiled them and that everyone should make their own luck. After Nunzio died, Felicia reentered the workforce and became successful. No one helped me, she thought. Of course, nothing could have been further from the truth. She had connected with an attorney in town who hired her, then assisted her in getting her job at the title company. She did not have to pay rent, and Angela and Franco helped her whenever she needed it.

"As I was saying at the apartment," Joe said. "I think my sister will die of a heart attack one day. And my stepmother, don't get me started on her."

"I want to go to college here," said Marie. She was hoping to interject herself into the conversation to keep the boredom at bay.

"Alicia called me last week asking me about the kids and how they were doing," said Felicia. "But I don't think she's actually interested."

"She's such a phony. I'm always giving her money, too."

"I said I'm going to college here," said Marie.

"If you get accepted," Felicia said.

Felicia and Joe continued with their intense conversation as if they were deciding the fate of the world. Next on the chopping block was her cousin, Alicia's daughter.

"Helena is a cold tomato. All she does is take—rarely gives anything. How is your food, Marie?" asked Joe. "I hope you like it."

"It's wonderful." Marie loved her uncle but made a mental note to never interact with people whose only conversation was gossip. It seemed that they needed to express all their frustrations in one communication before they exploded. Marie looked at her watch and prayed that they did not order dessert.

When Marie and Felicia got home, they knew Angela had made dinner from the aroma on the porch. Andrea and Frank were already sitting at the table. Angela was waiting for them with a homemade pizza.

"Felicia, I have dinner ready."

"How was your visit with Joe?" asked Angela.

"He's doing well," said Felicia. "He's getting ready for a trip to London."

"Did you enjoy yourself, Marie?" asked Angela.

"Wonderful. It's great being in the city. I'll be going to go to college there." She wanted to say that she had spent the day listening to two pent-up people who, to relieve their frustrations, shot energetic bullets at people with whom they disapproved.

"That is, if we can afford it," said Felicia. "I don't know why you want to do that."

"I think she wants to take a chance," said Angela, winking at Marie.

Felicia was silent. Angela put ideas in Marie's head that she thought were unstable. What if living in Manhattan did not work out. What then?

"If you do that," said Felicia. "Don't come crying to me if it doesn't work out. You'll need to make it on your own."

All of Felicia's children were independent thinkers, and she often chastised them, thinking that was a good thing. Felicia wanted to present herself as more conservative so the pendulum would not swing too far to the right or left. She believed balance should always be maintained, regardless of the situation and who was involved.

"I had to take a chance when I married your uncle. I made the choice to come to America and begin a new life, even though I did not know what to expect. The experiences that made up my new life were some of the hardest years of my life. No path is paved in gold, but now when I look at all of you, I can say that it was worth it."

"Thanks, Aunt Angela," said Marie.

Felicia wished Angela did not compare her former situation to present day. It was a different time and place. Her blatant acceptance of Marie's ideas interfered with Felicia's authority.

"On Monday I need to do a closing on a house in Yorktown," said Felicia. "I'll have to figure out how to get there."

"Be careful driving," said Angela.

After dinner, Angela put a Caruso record on the record player. The tenor sang "Santa Lucia," and Angela began to hum. She and Franco collected Caruso records over the years, and she still enjoyed the clear, powerful voice that sang about Italy and its sweet places. It was not that she was nostalgic or even wished to return; it was just a reminder of her past and how far she had come.

"What are you doing, Aunt Angela?" asked Marie. "I heard your Caruso record."

"I'm just cleaning up," said Angela. "You can do your homework at my desk in the sitting room if you want."

"I don't have much homework," said Marie. "Caruso must remind you of home."

"It's a reminder. This is my home, here with you. I'm glad you had a good time with your uncle," said Angela. "He had so little growing up. I'm glad he has a lot now."

"I know I'll live in New York someday," said Marie.

"As long as you are going to school," said Angela. "You have developed your vision. That is a good thing."

"Vision is not going to get me into college," said Marie.

"No, but you can use it in school to see beyond what most people see. That's how you stand out."

"What did you and your uncle talk about?" asked Angela.

"Uncle Joe and Mom talked about family stuff mostly. I went out for a walk. I really wasn't part of the conversation."

Angela was pleased with the relationship between Felicia and Joe. She felt it helped hold the family together, since Joe had an interest in family members and all the gossip. She had secretly not wanted Felicia to remarry so the children would remain at Morning Glory Avenue. Angela concerned herself with the children and did not meddle in Felicia's personal life. Sometimes the children would ask Angela if their mother had dates, and Angela would tell them that was their mother's concern and not the family's.

"Why didn't you stay and talk?"

"Because it was all gossip. I really wanted to go out in New York and have fun. They were talking about Aunt Alicia and her daughter. You should have seen them; it was as if someone had speeded up a film. They were so frenetic. Nobody wanted to talk about what I was doing or who I was, so I went to Bryant Park and the library."

"Try not to be so hard on your mother and uncle. They do their best. Next time, meet him for lunch by yourself."

"Why don't you come with me to see Uncle Joe?" asked Marie.

Angela had encouraged the relationship between Marie and Joe because she knew that Joe could provide an alternative to life in Nelsonville. She believed that to expand into a life of possibility, one needed to reach beyond the home environment. This was the opportunity Angela felt Marie needed.

"I'm too old to be walking around New York City," said Angela. "I've done my share of visiting the city. It is too noisy and dirty for me. Besides, my legs do not work the way they used to. I want you to benefit from the connection."

"I had a strange experience while I was there."

"What was it?"

"I closed my eyes, and I could see people who were dressed in old clothing— something out of the Victorian Age. They were superimposed on present day. It was brief, so there were not many details. It was like…"

"Staring into the mirror," said Angela.

"So, I can do this at will?"

"When you close your eyes, you can drift and see where it takes you, but remember you also live in the real world. You have to walk between them."

Marie felt liberated that her sight was not dependent on any object. The mirror was just a tool to access deeper knowledge and information.

"Once I get my early acceptance to college, I won't have to spend much time in classes, so I'll spend more time the in city."

"Look at these pictures," said Angela, walking over to the buffet. "This is Uncle Franco and me in front of our first house in Nelsonville. We lived there with your great-grandmother and your grandmother."

"You don't regret immigrating to America?"

"It was the right choice, even though there were many disappointments and tragedies. It was worth it because you were born, and I can help you live a good life and make the right choices. You kids are everything to me."

"We're lucky to have you, Aunt Angela," said Marie. "Anyway, can I make a sandwich to take with me tomorrow for school? Mom only has tuna upstairs."

"I have mozzarella and tomato," said Angela.

"That sounds good," said Marie. "You've led an exotic life. My life will look small in comparison."

"You can create your life the way you want. What do you want your life to be?"

"I can be adventurous and travel, meet new people, and be surprised where I end up."

"Within reason, I don't see why not. I hope you get everything you want. Now let's make your sandwich."

The world was now such a radically different place from Angela's youth that when she got impressions of the past, they were faded. Her attitude had changed toward fashion, personal relationships, and war.

She closed the front door, and the hall clock chimed 3pm. Knowing the kids would be home from school soon, she prepared biscotti and tea.

Andrea and Marie walked up the stairs to the side porch.

"Do you want something to eat?" asked Angela.

"No, tell Mom that I will be home when the streetlights come on," said Andrea. "I won't be home for dinner."

"You are not going out. I will call your mother at the office if you do that. Come in and have something to eat now. Eat all you want," said Angela. "You won't have dinner until your mother gets home."

"I won't be hungry for dinner," said Marie after eating some biscotti. "This is enough for me."

"You have to eat more. You don't want to get too skinny," Angela said.

"I don't want anything. I'm supposed to meet my friends," said Andrea.

Out of all four of the children, Andrea was the most rebellious. When Speranza's daughter Alicia insisted on marrying someone who had a reputation for abusing women, she married him anyway. Andrea had that same stubborn disposition of defiance. Angela had let Alicia slide, but she was not going to do that with Andrea.

"Andrea, go upstairs and start your homework and wait for your mother to come home or I'll have her come home now," said Angela.

Andrea stamped her feet all the way up the back stairs.

"Mom always has to keep on her," said Marie.

"Andrea has a temper," said Angela. "It's good she can stand up for herself, but she can get into trouble."

"I know. I can't believe she made it through Catholic school through the eighth grade. Did you have clients today?" asked Marie.

"No, I have two clients tonight. How was school?" asked Angela.

"Ok. Mostly just boring," said Marie. "I know college will be better."

"You will meet a lot of new people," said Angela. "You just have to have confidence."

"Did you ever doubt that you could make dresses for people?"

"No, after the quality of work I saw when I came to this country, I had no doubt that I would have clients. I had a story to tell along with my sewing abilities. Mrs. Einbinder, one of my clients, once said that she would write about my life. She was a playwright in Germany before she immigrated, but because of the war, it never happened. Maybe you will write it one day."

A bang came from upstairs.

"What's she doing up there?" asked Marie.

Angela opened the door to the back stairs. "Andrea, what are you doing? What fell?"

"The iron dropped," called Andrea. "I'm fine."

"Marie, go up and see what she is doing."

Marie went up the back stairs.

Angela thought about her nephew Robert and where he might be. She often worried about him. Angela heard Felicia's car pulling into the driveway and watched as she got out of the car and came up the side steps.

"Are the girls home?" asked Felicia. "Frank said he was staying in the city tonight."

"Upstairs. Andrea dropped an iron, so I don't know what she's doing up there."

"Any news from Robert?" asked Angela.

"I talked to a lawyer at work, and he has recommended a lawyer who takes on these cases if we need it—but I don't think we will. I made a few calls, and it seems that our Captain Bonifice has been receiving money from families whose sons want to avoid the draft."

"We'll have to invite him for that dinner."

Later that evening, Mrs. Einbinder came to a dress fitting. The Vietnam War was a topic discussed by the two women since its inception. Not everyone supported the war, and Mrs. Einbinder was happy that there were protests and outspoken dissention. Angela agreed and told Mrs. Einbinder about her nephew's plight.

"It's good that he's a conscientious objector," said Mrs. Einbinder. "If more young men left the country, then they would have less men to fight—and a strong statement would be made."

"World War II changed Nunzio," said Angela. "He really never came home. I tried to pretend that he was the same, but he was not."

"And now with the advanced weapons, it will be a lot worse for the men fighting this war," said Mrs. Einbinder.

"I wish Robert would let us know where he is," said Angela. "It would make me feel better."

"I'm sure he'll get in touch when it's safe," said Mrs. Einbinder.

Felicia came in the front door carrying a thick folder.

"What is that?" asked Angela.

"Work that I didn't get to today," said Felicia as she walked toward the stairs.

"Should we invite Captain Bonifice for dinner next week?"

"Definitely," Felicia nodded.

Chapter 3-
FOLLOWING THE PATH

"I don't blame them for not going to war," said Angela. "It's no way to live."

"We always had war in Europe," said Lizzy. "It was tough."

"Why do we want it to be tough here?" asked Angela. "Have we not had enough of war?"

"What do you mean? We can't let the Communists take over," said Lizzy as she cut herself another piece of cake. "They fight for our freedom."

"You don't believe that," said Angela. "They fight because our government wants something. The big corporations make money from war—become richer. We are no better than any country that wants more."

Angela was forthright with her ideas with Sadie and Lizzy; the rest of the Italian-American community tended to be more closed-minded and ultra conservative. Angela felt Lizzy was repeating what she was told as a young person and sensed that she did not believe the words in her heart.

"I hope Robert comes home and the authorities leave him alone," said Lizzy. "I know you and Felicia must be worried. The government is powerful, and they do what they want."

"Robert always was a free spirit," Angela said as she poured tea.

"We have to be who we are," said Lizzy. "People find out anyway."

"That depends on how much you want them to find out," Angela said.

Angela heard someone running down the back stairs. The door swung open and Marie appeared.

"My bread dough is rising; please don't run down the stairs," said Angela. "The dough will fall." She often put her rising dough in the back stairway.

"Sorry, Aunt." Marie kissed Angela on the cheek. Angela held Marie's chin and kissed her on both cheeks.

"I love you," said Angela. "I love that you are simpatico. Going to school today?"

Marie had planned to take the early morning train to New York. It was Friday, and she was tired of boring classes.

"Yeah, on my way," said Marie. "Early visit today, Lizzy."

"Oh, yeah. I don't sleep much."

"Are you sure?" asked Angela. "You do not have any books."

"They're in my locker," said Marie.

"All of them?" asked Angela.

Marie saw that Angela knew she was either going to New York or horseback riding at the dude ranch. Angela's lifted chin and raised eyebrows let Marie know that she was waiting for a better story.

"Well, ok," said Marie. "I thought I'd go into New York and visit City College. I should get to know the campus and see what goes on."

"You have been there, and students are going to class," said Angela. "That is what is going on."

"Please don't say anything," said Marie. "It seems like a waste of time to go to class here."

"If you spend the day with me while I visit some friends, then my lips will not tell your secret," said Angela. "This will be our special secret."

"Fine." Marie smiled.

"I'd better get home so you two can start your day," said Lizzy as she leaned on the table and pushed herself to her feet.

Angela disappeared into her bedroom. Marie hopped up on the platform that stood in front of her aunt's dressmaking mirror in the hall, which reminded her of a platform for a statue that you would see in museums.

Marie confidently projected her awareness into the mirror. She felt a rush of energy from the mirror pulling her into the reflected space. She entered the looking glass's space with a swish, and its vastness embraced her. She assumed that everyone had their own personal experience when they entered the portal. Marie was alone in the white empty environment with a tinge of sunny yellow that surrounded her like a blanket. The warmth of the yellow felt uplifting and safe until it was swept away and morphed into a dark blue ocean with high waves in the distance. The wakes pushed her over. As quickly as she was pushed over, she found herself on her feet again. The waves came closer and closer, and they were about to envelop her.

"Are you ready to go?" asked Angela.

The force of the water pushed her back in her body again. She shook her head and refocused her eyes and found herself in the present. They walked up Morning Glory Avenue away from town and past houses that were built in the 1930s and 1940s. Marie drove past these houses regularly with her mother but hardly noticed them.

"Where are we going?" asked Marie.

"Just a few more blocks," said Angela.

Angela held Marie's elbow as they walked. They were silent as they sauntered, seeming to float above the sidewalk and allowing their connection to move them along.

"I want to show you a house," said Angela.

"Do we know the people who live there?"

"No, not now."

"So, we're not going inside?"

"Stop asking so many questions," said Angela. "You do not always have to know where you are going. Let it be a mystery."

"Mystery? I could be in the city enjoying Greenwich Village. I never know who I will meet, but I know where I'm going. That is a mystery." Marie was taught by both the

educational system and her mother that you had to know where
you were going and what you were going to do once you got
there. It was not comfortable to be in limbo.

"Here it is," said Angela.

"What, this house? Why are we here?"

"Your Uncle Franco built this house," said Angela.

"He built it?"

"He designed it and hired people to do the work. He did a
lot of work on it himself."

"I didn't know he built this house."

"An important man in town hired him to create it," said
Angela. "Your uncle could do anything."

The house was gray with a rounded porch that stretched
around the back. There were three floors with a small balcony
off the second floor.

"It's different from our house. Why didn't he build
something similar?"

"Because our house was built in 1888. That kind of
construction is too expensive today. Our stained-glass windows
were imported. This is what people could afford in the 1930s. It
was during the Depression."

Marie thought it elegant in its simplicity.

"How could anyone afford to build this during the
Depression? It seems that you and Uncle Franco always had
work during the Depression, while many were in bread lines."

"We have always been independent since we came to this
country. We had a garden and our own chickens, and our
clients were loyal. There is always work around somewhere.
Then the Second World War came and pulled us out of the
Depression."

"The war pulled us out?"

"Yes, many prospered during the war, especially those
who sold tanks and other war equipment to the Nazis. Most
Americans had no idea. The war brought more employment for
everyone."

"It must be common knowledge that he made money from
equipment that killed America soldiers."

"You would think so, but everyone was so united during WWII that it did not make headlines."

"That's outrageous. They don't teach that in history class."

"It's all about making money," Angela said. "They won't teach that in school."

"No one protested? People must have known."

"It was not common knowledge," Angela said. Remember it was the 1940s, and the patriotic spirit was at its height."

Marie took a deep breath and looked at the house.

Are there fireplaces in this house?" asked Marie.

"Just a small one made of brick in the living room."

"How long did it take to build?" asked Marie.

"About a year. I love walking by here and seeing your uncle's work. This was his vision. He loved our house, but he did not build it."

"Amazing he could bring this house into form. He didn't have any training as an architect?"

"No, but he was persistent and practiced all the right skills," said Angela. "He also knew people who would help him."

"Why didn't you show me this house before?"

"You are able to appreciate it now. Besides, soon you will be in college and it will challenge your persistence. Like this house, you can build a solid foundation; then you will be successful. This house has been here for almost forty years."

Marie often felt exasperated with her aunt when she was obtuse. Angela's life lessons were buried in storytelling, but Marie felt she should be more forthright.

"So, I should build a solid foundation. Is that what you're saying?"

"I think with persistence and study, you can achieve your goals. You should not be afraid of anything. Your uncle had never built a house on his own before, but he did it. You come from a long line of builders. It just takes time."

"I don't really know what my goals are exactly. I know I love history and would like to major in that subject."

"I think that would suit you."

Angela hugged Marie and thought about Speranza, her sister-in-law. Speranza had little opportunity in life, and now her granddaughter was planning a life that would have been entirely out of the question for her grandmother. Even Angela's own experience as a business owner was something that would have been unachievable had she stayed in Sicily. Angela would often tell herself that her father would have been proud of what she had achieved in America. She remembered her father bringing home remnants of silk from his travels and her mother making garments and linens. To this day, Angela still made her own tablecloths and napkins.

"What do you think?" asked Angela.

Marie stared at the ground in silence.

"About the house?"

"That or anything that comes to mind. What are you thinking about?"

"Well… I had another experience, or it was kind of an experience and I'm not sure…"

"Speak up," said Angela.

"I had an experience with the mirror again before we left," said Marie.

"Did you stare into the mirror?" asked Angela. "What did you see?"

"Everything was fine at first, but then there were rough waves that almost got me. It was like they spit me out of the mirror."

"Sounds like the energies were testing you."

"Testing me? For what?"

"Maybe for the next part of your life. To see how strong you are. To see if you can tolerate the current. Sometimes I think of the images as a reflection of what is inside us."

"What else could I see in there?"

"You have to be prepared for things that could frighten you," said Angela.

"Are dead people in there?" asked Marie. "You talk to people who are dead."

"Do not say that out loud," Angela said. "People will condemn you. Keep it to yourself."

"Uncle Joe said you used to talk to his mother after she died, and you talk to the Virgin Mary. You have an altar devoted to her."

"I never discuss my connections with the world we cannot see unless it is necessary. It is best that way, and I think you should do the same. Look forward, not in the past. It is time to go home," said Angela. "You need to go to school."

They walked a block in silence. Angela wondered if she should explore deeper into what Marie saw. She did not want to open Pandora's box. She wanted her niece to move ahead in her life unencumbered, but she could not hold back.

"What do you think the waves were about?" asked Angela.

"I don't know," said Marie. "It was like coming home at first. There were lots of colors and a warmth coming from the mirror. But then there were high waves that shoved me out of the mirror. It was strange."

"Maybe what was in the mirror did not want you there, or your experience was finished."

"Could you always talk to the dead? Why don't you talk about it more?"

"I have had a connection to the unseen world since I was a child, and I learned to be careful who I shared it with. I told a priest once when I was child that I talked to people who had died and wanted to communicate with the living. He told me I was blasphemous and to say an entire rosary, and then he told my mother what I had said. She said it was the work of the devil and I was never to speak of it again. You should be aware with whom you share your experiences. The church thinks it has a monopoly on spiritual communication," Angela said. "They're used to people going through them."

For more than fifty years, Angela's clients had stood in front of her mirror. Maybe the mirror's interior landscape was affected by who stood in front of it, she thought. Her clients came from various backgrounds: Jewish, Italian, American. She had clients who had been with her for a few years, others who had used her services for the decades since she'd started her business. Maybe their histories were embedded in the mirror. She often thought about her plan for the mirror when she retired from making garments for the public—how she would take it to the backyard and smash it, then bury it next to her garden. The ghosts of the past would be set free.

"Do I have to go to school? I could still catch a train to the city," said Marie.

"Make an appearance at school," said Angela. "Just show your face, please. We have enough trouble with your brother Robert. Do that for me and your mother. And do not talk to the dead; talk to the living."

"All right," said Marie. "But tomorrow I'm going to the city all day."

"You always have to have the last word," said Angela. "That is not always necessary. Just keep your focus and build a strong foundation."

Showing Marie Franco's construction was an intuitive act. Her nephews Frank and Robert knew about the house, but it was more profound to show Marie what could be accomplished when one took risks. Angela had become successful beyond her dreams by coming to the United States, but the nuns had given her the appropriate foundation.

Marie entered the front door at Nelsonville High School and went to her locker, expecting another monotonous day. She straightened her yellow linen dress and walked down the hall.

"Oh, Marie, I haven't seen you in a while," said Alice, one of Marie's friends.

"Yeah, I have had to take care of my aunt. Sometimes she doesn't feel well, and we don't want to leave her alone."

"You're not a good friend. You ignore us, and honestly, we were all saying how weird you are. My father works in the city and he says he sees you sometimes going into Manhattan, so maybe your aunt isn't unwell. That's weird."

"I'm really sorry." Marie felt she was in the wrong and that she needed to repent for her absence. Maybe she should make more of an effort.

"If you're really sorry, you'll wash all the blackboards at the end of school today. I was assigned to wash them because of some little mishap. If you do that, then you're back in with our group."

"All right." She felt she could not say no. It was just a way of placating a dissatisfied energy.

"You're the best," said Alice as she walked away.

"Is anyone getting together after school?" called Marie. Alice did not turn around. Marie froze in her position and looked around to see if anyone overheard. She observed everyone chatting and going to class and did not understand the connection they all had.

"Hello," said Angela as she picked up the hall phone. "It's me," said Robert.

"Robert, my God, we have been so worried," said Angela. "It's been six months. Where are you?"

"I can't say, but I just wanted to let you know I'm okay."

"The FBI came here."

"That's why I can't tell you where I am. Is everyone alright?"

"Yes, fine. Your mother is at work. You should call her."

"Just tell her I'm ok and working to get home."

"When will you be home?"

"As soon as I can," said Robert.

Angela heard a click, then silence.

"Hello, hello," said Angela.

Angela hung up and called Felicia to tell her about Robert. At least they knew he was safe and would eventually come home. If he needed a lawyer, Felicia had connections in town with the best attorneys, but first she would invite Captain Bonifice to dinner. Everything will be all right, thought Angela. She felt the worry lift from her shoulders, and the energy that had been blocked with concern began to return. It was not a jolt but a steady brightening of the cells of her body.

Angela took a deep breath and began to plan a Sunday luncheon for family and friends. It was time, she thought. In the time since Franco died and the issues with Robert and the draft, she had felt suppressed and defeated, but now she felt she had turned a corner and a barrier had been broken. Robert would not have the experience of war that his father suffered. Robert would come home, and the unpopular Vietnam War would end. She went into the kitchen to make a list of what she would need for her luncheon.

Chapter 4

SUNDAY LUNCHEON
AND THE AFTERMATH

Angela and Felicia were preparing lunch on a cold, sunny Sunday. The menu consisted of antipasto, gnocchi, pan-fried fish, and roasted vegetables. Angela did not invite the number of guests she would have invited when Franco was alive. This was her party, and she invited those who were closest to her—not people who were part of a certain segment of the Italian-American community. Marie, Andrea, and Frank, friends Sadie Malaci, and Lizzy Liamonte, would be there. In addition to the regular guests was guest of honor Captain Arthur Bonifice, veteran and colleague of Nunzio's at Camp Smith who had remained in the reserves. His connections were rumored to extend to the top echelons of the military.

Sadie and Lizzie were good for a laugh, and the captain would see how Nunzio's children had grown with ambitions to contribute to the world. The perfect storm for success in Angela's mind.

Felicia and her three children settled in at the table as Angela situated herself at the table's end.

"Captain Bonifice, sit next to me," said Angela. "Our other guests will be here shortly." She wanted to make sure that she could have an intimate conversation with the captain. Felicia sat on the other side of him.

"I'm between two lovely ladies," said the captain.

"We thought we would catch up," said Felicia.

"Yes," said Angela, "it has been too long."

"The children have grown," said the captain. "How are you doing, Frank? You are in college?"

"Yeah, NYU. Electrical engineering program. I'm living at home until I graduate."

"Have you thought about joining up once you graduate? I can get you what you want."

The captain had had a distinguished military career. He had been awarded the Legion of Merit, Soldier's Medal, and the Purple Heart. On this occasion, the captain was in plain clothes.

"Where is Robert?" asked the captain.

"He's probably in Canada," said Andrea.

"This is a lot of food," said Marie. "Are you planning to put us in a coma?"

Felicia shot her a look that could split ice.

"Many so-called "conscientious objectors" run to Canada instead of facing up to their responsibilities," said the captain.

"I don't see why young men should take on the responsibility of the government and their greed," Angela said. "Maybe Robert is visiting friends in Canada."

"I imagine he's been drafted," the captain said.

The front door opened and shut. A mumbled conversation could be heard coming from the foyer.

"Hi, everybody, sorry we're late. It was Lizzy's fault," said Sadie.

"What are you saying, it's my fault," said Lizzy. "You were late picking me up."

"Sit down, sit down," said Angela. "Lizzy, Sadie this is Captain Bonifice, a good friend of Nunzio's. They worked at Camp Smith together."

Angela and Felicia went into the kitchen.

"Oh, you're a captain," said Sadie. "You're not in your uniform today. Men always look so nice in a uniform."

"I'm in the reserves."

"The captain has a lot of medals," said Marie.

"Frank, how are you doing in college?" asked Sadie.

"Well, I'm already looking at companies that would hire me once I graduate."

"That is nice," said Lizzie. "Good to look ahead."

Sadie sat next to the captain.

"I believe Felicia is sitting here," the captain said.

"Oh, what a shame," said Sadie. "I thought we could get better acquainted."

Captain Bonifice laughed but seemed unsure about Sadie's subtle intent.

"Here we are," said Angela as she entered the room. Felicia and Angela placed bowls and plates of pasta and chicken parmagiana.

"Pass the platters," said Felicia.

Angela and Felicia were going to wait until after lunch to talk to the captain, but it seemed he suspected that something was amiss with Andrea's remark about Canada.

"I think we should all eat," said Lizzy. "As you can tell by my size, I love to eat."

"You can say that again," said Sadie, draining her wine glass. "See, kids, this is what happens when you're Italian and eat too much pasta."

Everyone laughed. This was exactly why Angela had invited Sadie and Lizzy. They could be counted on to derail a conversation that was going in an undesirable direction. Angela knew the cat was out of the bag, and now she would have to delicately navigate the captain into a conversation that would benefit Robert.

"I hope you like chicken parmigiana, Captain," Felicia said. "I remembered you enjoyed it."

"Yes," said the captain, "I think you served it the last time I was here."

"That's right," said Angela. "We always enjoyed your company. We have paid attention to the progression of your career."

"I'm flattered," the captain said.

After everyone ate, Angela decided that she needed to clear the dining room.

"Kids, I have cannoli in the kitchen," said Angela. "Why don't you grab one before you leave?"

"Sounds good," said Andrea and left the dining room.

"We're leaving?" asked Marie.

Frank and Marie sat and waited.

"Are you done?" asked Felicia.

"Aren't you bringing them out?" Marie asked.

Angela tilted her head toward the kitchen. Frank and Marie looked at each other and Marie sighed. They got up and went into the kitchen.

"When you leave, go out the back door," called Felicia.

"Oh sure, we have to leave by the service entrance," shouted Marie.

Felicia gave the captain a slight smile while restraining herself from getting up and chastising Marie for her backtalk.

"Kids," said Felicia, "they always have something to say."

"Lizzy and I are on diets, so we need to leave. It's just too tempting," said Sadie as she winked at Angela.

"We are?" asked Lizzy.

"Yes, remember I told you that we weren't having dessert today. Thank you, Angela and Felicia. Captain, it was nice to meet you."

She assisted Lizzy on with her coat and escorted her out the front door.

"We were thinking, Arthur," said Angela, using his first name, "you might be able to help us bring Robert home."

"I cannot get involved with a draft dodger," said Arthur, having surmised the truth. "It would stain my reputation."

Angela paused and decided to push the conversation further before she presented him with her information about the funds he'd received for "helping" other parents keep their sons safe.

"I'm sure Nunzio would want you to help Robert, since you both fought in WWII and he worked with you at Camp Smith," said Felicia.

"That may be so, but I hesitate to do that since so many young men are fighting and dying in Vietnam. I can't give someone special treatment."

Angela thought quickly about how to proceed.

"You know, Arthur, I have many wealthy dressmaking clients, and several had young sons of draft age. Felicia informed me that their sons somehow obtained deferments. They said that there was a captain in the reserves at Camp Smith who helped them. Maybe there is a captain that you know of that assisted these men?"

Angela and Felicia had worked together to find information about Captain Bonifice. They were of like mind. They respected the military, but when it came to family, military rules did not apply.

"I…I'm sure their deferments were warranted," said Arthur, his face turning red. He had no idea how these two women could have knowledge of his dealings at Camp Smith.

"Do you know who that might be?" asked Felicia. "I could contact him."

The captain adjusted himself in his seat, tilted his head and looked off in the distance. Angela knew Arthur would now cooperate.

"Is that seat uncomfortable?" asked Angela. "I can get you a pillow."

"There is no need to call," said Captain Bonifice. "I can take care of this."

"That would be wonderful, Arthur," said Angela.

"Yes, it would be," said Felicia.

"I will bring out the dessert," said Angela. "Something sweet always makes the day better—easier to swallow the difficulties in life."

"You know, I am so full I don't think I could eat another bite," said Arthur.

"What a shame," said Angela.

"Thank you, but I need to be going," said Arthur. He stood up and asked for his jacket.

"Thank you for helping Robert," said Angela.

"I will put that deferment in tomorrow. It may take a month."

Both women walked the captain to the front door.

"Remember to come by anytime," said Angela.

Angela closed the door behind him.

"Well Felicia, that will be the last time we'll see him until he's laid out in a casket."

The front door burst open.

"I see that Captain Bonifice left," said Marie. "He hurried to his car and mumbled goodbye. Did you ladies scare him? What did you say?"

"Nothing," said Angela. "Everything will be all right now."

Angela had encountered many barriers to her goals in the past, some of which she could not surmount. When Speranza's daughter, Alicia, wanted to marry an abusive man, Angela was against the match and tried to steer her toward someone more appropriate. When she failed to prevent the marriage, she helped her niece as much as she could, but she felt thwarted at every turn. Though Alicia did leave her husband, she would eventually return to the abusive relationship.

Nunzio's children had more direction in life. Not that there would no longer be obstacles, but it was possible to dissolve them. Captain Bonifice was a powerful man with even more powerful contacts, but with a little information applied strategically, any resistance melted.

The next morning, Sadie Malaci climbed the porch stairs.

"Hi, Sadie," said Felicia. "Angela is in the house."

"Good to see you, Sadie," said Marie.

"Good to see you too, kid."

"Oh, I forgot you were coming," said Angela as she opened the front door.

"I didn't think I was that forgettable," said Sadie.

"I see Felicia and Marie are going on an outing," said Sadie. "Are they getting along any better? I hope none of them have sharp objects with them."

"Felicia is going to work, and Marie is pretending to go to school. Come in the kitchen."

"How is Marie doing?" asked Sadie.

"She is doing well," said Angela. "All of Nunzio's children are doing well."

"Did Captain Bonifice react to your request? Did you have to pull out the big guns?"

"I just reminded him about a captain that was paid off by rich families so their sons did not have to go to war. I asked him to help Robert, but he said he was not comfortable doing that for a draft dodger—so I simply said some of my clients had used a captain's services to release their sons from the draft and that I would ask them the captain's name. He became accommodating after that." She put the espresso pot on the stove.

"You're a smooth operator, Angela. A woman after my own heart."

"Captain Bonifice was good friends with Nunzio," said Angela. "I just reminded him of that friendship." They both laughed.

"I'm sure you reminded him," said Sadie. "Brava."

To Angela, that was the difference between mainstream America and European immigrant communities: immigrants were not naive about how things worked for people in power, and they knew how to turn things around to benefit those with less power. Angela thought of her dealings with Captain Bonifice like a recipe: she reminded the captain of his friendship with her nephew, and if that did not work then she would have had to add more pepper or oregano to obtain the desired result. You just lay on more information, highly effective in its simplicity.

"If I ever need to get out of anything, I'll remember to call on you. You don't fear powerful people. Do you have any whiskey to put in this coffee?"

Marie lay on her side, hand supporting her head, on her mother's bed as Felicia got ready to go out.

"What do you want to do after high school?" asked Felicia. Felicia put on her black pumps and dress.

"I'm going to college," said Marie. "What else would I do?"

"You could get a job. What will be your major?" asked Felicia.

"I don't know. I'll figure it out. I have time."

"You need to major in something practical," said Felicia.

Nunzio's death had taught Felicia to be prepared for any unexpected occurrence, so a marketable skill was essential.

"I certainly will," said Marie. "I just have to figure out which major will afford me the best results."

Marie was as adept as her mother and aunt at navigating challenging situations and turning them in her favor.

"That's more like it," said Felicia. "I like to see a return on my investment."

Marie smiled reassuringly at her mother. She never told Felicia about her experience with the mirror because her mother would scold her for being too flighty—or worse, committing blasphemy. Felicia attended Catholic mass every Sunday, and every Sunday she financially contributed to the church.

"Do you get a return on investment when you give money to the church? They did not even help you when dad died."

"What do you mean? I give to the church for upkeep."

"They said they would help you find a job after Dad died, and the best they came up with was a cleaning lady job. They did not consider that you had an education, which tells me they don't know who you are."

"You need to watch your mouth. It is none of your business who I give money to and for what reason."

Marie knew that her mother did not take the cleaning job offered because she was confident enough to know she could do better. Marie sensed Felicia hid her true feelings about the church, but appearance was everything.

The energy surrounding Marie's relationship with her mother was bumpy, while her relationship with Angela flowed. They understood one another, and it was Angela's storytelling that would influence Marie's academic and life choices.

"Where are you going?" asked Marie.

"One of the girls in the office is having a get-together."

"Sounds like fun," said Marie. "Have a good time." Marie knew that her mother would be in an elevated mood for a few days after she had socialized.

Felicia turned toward a mirror and put on her pearl earrings.

"Mom, do you ever go on dates?" asked Marie.

Felicia met Marie's eyes in the mirror.

"Is that any of your business?" asked Felicia.

"Well…I guess not," said Marie, thinking it better to keep her in a good mood.

"That's better," said Felicia as she adjusted her dress.

Felicia sprayed her perfume in the air and walked into the aroma. The scent hung in the air. Marie breathed it in. It was the same with her Uncle Joe's cologne. Every time he visited the house on Morning Glory Avenue, the scent lingered for a day or so.

"Don't forget to do your homework," called Felicia.

In the spring of 1969, like a miracle, Robert quietly came home with a deferment, and everything had quieted down except that he was adrift in a sea of confusion. Angela came upstairs with folded laundry over her arm and saw that Robert was rolling tobacco. She interpreted that to mean he had no money for cigarettes.

"Marie, go to the store and buy your brother cigarettes," said Angela. "He's rolling his own. Here's the money."

"Aunt Angela, he's not rolling tobacco; he's rolling weed. You don't have to buy him cigarettes."

"Go get him cigarettes so he'll have them. He has no money."

"He's selling weed. He has money," said Marie.

Regardless of whether Angela knew what Robert was selling, her intent was from her heart—to make life easier for Robert.

"Okay, I'll go. What brand do you want, Robert?" asked Marie.

"Get me some Marlboros, I guess," said Robert. He drew in on his joint and his eyes relaxed, his dark curly hair framed his face.

"You're a jerk," said Marie. She smoked marijuana occasionally but did not find it particularly enlightening or satisfying. With her developed intuition and discernment, getting high did not serve a purpose, although it did make everything more amusing. She left on her mission to buy cigarettes.

"Robert, you have to get a job doing something," said Angela.

"I'm doing okay selling tobacco," said Robert.

In fact, Robert had started selling marijuana in high school and had expanded his reach to New York City. He had even expanded his business to Canada during his time there, and he'd brought business associates on board. Felicia and Nunzio's children were nothing if not resourceful, regardless of their situation. Success was built into their future.

"My model is based on your service business, Aunt Angela," said Robert. "Thank you. I owe it all to you." He took a drag and settled back in his chair. "I like to test each shipment."

"Well, as long as you are not smoking all the profits," said Angela.

"No, I have pretty good profits."

After breathing in the smoke, Angela felt a bit ungrounded. She left the laundry on top of Felicia's bed and went downstairs. Angela made sure she helped Felicia with household chores so that when she came home from work there was nothing she had to do. Sometimes she made dinner for the entire family, when her own client schedule allowed.

Angela sat at her sewing machine and threaded the needle. She pulled the thread through and began to hem a dress she had created. She glanced at the full-length mirror and thought about the stories and conversations trapped inside—remembrances preserved for someone to tap into and learn about the people who lived these memories. Maybe the image of herself standing in front of the full-length mirror at the convent in her wedding dress still existed inside the glass. Not everyone could tap into the mirror's world; the seer needed to be fearless and open to unseen energies.

She shook herself out of her daydreaming and concentrated on the sewing. Pulling the garment through the sewing machine, she finished the hem. Years ago, it would have taken her over an hour to hem a dress by hand. She hung the garment on the edge of the mirror and caught her reflection in the glass.

"Hi, Aunt Angela," said Marie, returning with Robert's Marlboros. "Whose dress is that?"

"A new customer," said Angela. "What are you doing today?"

"Since it's Saturday, I thought I would go riding," said Marie.

"Remember your posture when you are riding," said Angela. "This way the horse will pay attention."

"It's a dude ranch, Aunt Angela. Nobody pays attention to posture; they just sit in the saddle."

"I am saying that posture is important. People and animals trust you more. Never cower."

Angela took any opportunity she could to teach and improve the lives of everyone around her. She sensed that Marie would lead a more unusual life than her contemporaries for which she needed to develop a strong spine. Whenever a memory was triggered, Angela would share the lesson, even if that person did not listen.

"Where do you get these ideas?" asked Marie.

"Things I have learned over the years. It is best to say them out loud."

Angela had spent the first years in America keeping her opinions to herself, which in retrospect, she felt had been a mistake. She remembered when she and Franco bought the house on Morning Glory Avenue and they hosted their first dinner party. The guests were Italian immigrants who had worked diligently, endured many hardships in America, and built successful businesses. The ideas expressed at the dinner were politically conservative in nature. All the opinions were communicated by the men, while the women nodded.

Angela had remained silent for fear of angering her guests and Franco. She and Franco had not been married long, and she was unsure of her position.

"Woodrow Wilson has hit us with too many taxes," said Gianni Galluci, the tailor.

"He sure has," said Franco.

"I have built my business from the bottom up," said Paolo Mancuso. "I am not giving my money to the government. We need a Republican in the presidency. Someone who understands business."

At that time, Angela had started to do sewing work for St. Mary's Episcopal School and was introducing herself to the community. The nuns paid her in cash, so there was no need to pay taxes. In fact, as she developed her clientele, they too paid her in cash. She did not see herself as a businesswoman, but as she built her customer base, she remained an undeclared business. She made her living through her creativity, and she could not imagine herself having a nine-to-five job.

"I agree," said Franco. "People need to find jobs and take care of themselves. The government cannot do everything."

Angela believed there could be a safety net for the unfortunate. She had been given a second chance through the generosity of The Sisters of Charity after the earthquake. Had she not had that safety net, she would have ended up begging on the street, or worse. The truth was that Angela and Franco ultimately helped many immigrants who arrived in America, regardless of political orientation or social situation. They were the most generous among the Italian community in Nelsonville.

Angela currently extended that generosity through sharing life lessons to those who would or would not listen. She simply shared her experience, seen or unseen.

"I wondered if you would come to St. Mary's School with me before you ride," said Angela.

"Don't tell me Uncle Franco built a building for the Episcopal nuns," joked Marie.

"No, I have some work to do there, and I think the Mother Superior would like to see you. Remember I used to bring you there when you were a little girl?"

"Yes, I remember. I loved going there."

"I know you did. Now you may have a new perception," Angela said. "We can leave now. It will not take long."

"I suppose. I'm not meeting anyone; I just thought I would take a leisurely ride on the trails."

They walked the hill up to St. Mary's, pausing occasionally to talk about the different houses they passed.

"When I came here, these houses were rented by Italians," said Angela. "Franco owned two of them and rented to new immigrants. They paid reduced rent for managing the houses, making sure the landscape was kept up and all appliances worked. It helped people get started in this country and brought us extra income."

"I guess that was smart," Marie said. "How did you get connected to an Episcopal school and convent?"

"Your uncle was doing jobs for the nuns when I came to this country, and they hired me, too."

They made their way onto St. Mary's School property. Marie remembered a small pond on the property where she had spent time sitting and taking in the foliage and wildlife, especially the tadpoles.

"I want to go by the pond," said Marie.

"All right," said Angela. "Meet me inside near the sewing room. You know where it is."

Marie thought she must have been nine or ten years old when she last sat beside the pond and focused on her reflection in the water. Her image reflected a delicate creature with an ethereal presence, and it felt incongruous to her surroundings in Nelsonville. Angela always stressed that she should be herself, but with Marie's sensibility that would be more challenging than Angela would have thought.

On this day, Marie sat and waited for the same feeling to overtake her, but it was not happening. Whatever happened to the magic? she wondered. I'm in the same place; why is it different? She leaned over and gazed at her reflection in the pond and saw that her face was clearly defined, even though the water was murky. She smiled into the water and waited. It was a bit like the mirror experience, as her vision started to morph and shift. Light figures came forward, and dark figures receded into the depths of the pond. The water was tranquil and still as glass, with the reflection of the trees, sky and birds like animated landscape painting. As the frogs croaked, Marie stared into the pond's murky deepness beyond the reflected scene. The sound of a bullfrog came from across the pond, and Marie looked up. A family of frogs sat on a rock and observed her.

"What are you looking at?" asked Marie. "There's not much privacy here anymore."

"Who are you talking to?"

Marie turned around and saw a nun standing near a tree.

"Your aunt is waiting for you," said the nun. "Mother Superior would like to see you."

Marie walked toward the school and glanced back at the pond, feeling a lingering bit of peace.

The Mother Superior and her aunt stood under a painting of the Blessed Virgin, dressed in a blue cape that swirled around her while her hands were in prayer position. She was looking down at her feet, where she stood on a serpent. The energy around the figure was dynamic, while Mary's face was serene and confident.

Marie recalled seeing this painting when she visited the school as a child with her aunt. It had felt like the image jumped off the canvas, communicating a message, soft but forceful. Seeing it again made her feel calm and relevant. Angela proudly reintroduced Marie to the Mother Superior.

"Sister Anna Claire, you remember my niece, Marie," said Angela. "She enjoyed it here as a child, and I wanted to show her St. Mary's School today."

Marie felt she was having a perfect day and one that she would draw on for much of her life.

"My, you have grown," said the Mother Superior. "I remember you as a little girl."

"Yes, Mother, and I remember you," said Marie.

"Angela, you must be very proud," said the nun.

Sister Anna Claire was the youngest Mother Superior in the history of St. Mary's School. She was known to be progressive in her ideas and appreciated art and music. The members of her order admired her determination to bring her school into the twentieth century and remain current and relevant. Marie's experience of nuns in the local Catholic school had been radically different. The nuns' ideology was conservative and remained rooted in nineteenth century thought, with little critical thinking. Her Uncle Joe had gone to the same school and experienced the same limitations and closed-mindedness. Marie had felt that the entire focus of her Catholic education was to control people's behavior and prevent them from being who they were. She did not get that feeling from St. Mary's School.

"I am so proud. She is planning an early acceptance to City College in New York."

"I think the city will suit you, Marie," said the nun. "You seem to be adventurous."

"Oh, I am. I want to travel someday and see Europe," said Marie. This is my kind of nun, she thought.

"What is your major?" asked the Mother Superior.

"I'm not sure yet," said Marie. "I'm hoping I can make a decision by the time I graduate in a few years."

Everyone expected her to know what she wanted to do, but the truth was that she would have to take classes and see which ones most interested her.

"I have heard that Nelsonville High School is not a good place for thinking people and young people who are adventurous," said the nun.

"It's not a place that I like. I just want to get my diploma and go off to college."

"And when you do, never look back," said the nun.

"Mother, show me what you need done," said Angela.

"First, let me show you something. Right this way."

The Mother Superior reached into her habit and took out a chain of keys and unlocked a room off her office.

"Come in," said the nun.

Angela and Marie inched their way into the nun's private space.

"Mother, how beautiful," said Angela.

The room was painted bright white and with an altar against the wall and a church kneeler in front for contemplation and prayer. Tall taper candles sat on pillars surrounding the statue of the Blessed Mother in her usual blue garb. Two gargoyles sat on each side of the altar. One was the image of a dragon crouching and gazing beyond the altar, as if looking out for enemies in the distance. The other was a monkey-like image with wings, resting his head in his hand as if contemplating the landscape before him.

"That is an unusual altar to our Blessed Mother," said Angela.

"Are you referring to my gargoyles?" asked the Mother Superior, smiling.

"Yes, I have never seen anything like them on a holy altar," said Angela. "Why are they on the altar, Mother, and what are they?" Angela remembered seeing similar creatures adorning the exterior of churches in Europe but did not know why they were there. To her they were grotesque.

"These gargoyles are modeled after the gargoyles on Notre Dame in Paris," said the nun. "They are on my altar to scare off evil and to guide and protect all who kneel at this altar. They are here to protect all that is feminine."

"They're amazing," said Marie. "I would like to see Notre Dame someday."

"I am sure you will," said the nun, smiling at Marie.

"They are so frightening," said Angela. "They are ugly things."

"During the Middle Ages, they were meant to inspire fear and express the horror of Hell to the masses and encourage people to come inside the church where salvation awaited them."

"And they had a practical purpose as well. They were spouts for draining rainwater, and some say they act as guides and one can consult with them about everyday life struggles."

"So, they had many meanings," said Marie.

"We should get some for your altar, Aunt Angela," said Marie.

"Angela, you have an altar?" asked the nun.

"Yes, like yours, it is an altar honoring the Blessed Mother. I have it because the Blessed Mother saved my life many years ago. But I do not have gargoyles."

"Well, the Blessed Mother does perform miracles," said the Mother Superior. "If you need protection, gargoyles are excellent to have. I have a sense that your altar is well protected and not in need of gargoyles."

Angela tried to resonate with the essence of the gargoyles, but she still found them to be too eerie to be on such a delicate altar. Throughout the years, she had consulted with her unseen friends for guidance about her life, so it was not different from what the Mother Superior was experiencing with the gargoyles; it was a matter of connection to the divine.

"We thank you for sharing your altar," said Angela. "I have mine in my bedroom, out of public view. I see that you are doing the same."

"One's private spiritual experience should be kept in solitude, away from prying eyes where an outsider may misconstrue the message," the Mother Superior said. "Don't you agree?"

"Yes, I completely agree," said Angela. Angela instinctively knew to hide her altar from view. It was a deeply personal experience to honor a connection to a divine entity. People usually prayed to deities, but the Blessed Mother was a woman chosen by God—a human with supernatural powers. Angela was comforted to know that she was acquainted with a like-minded practitioner. She felt her spiritual beliefs that were outside of church doctrine were not to be revealed or discussed.

Her connection to her unseen friends was deep alchemy and should be practiced privately.

"Let's go back into my office and I will show you what I need created," said the nun.

"Of course," said Angela. "Come, Marie."

"Can't I stay and look at the altar?"

"Certainly not. That is the Mother Superior's," said Angela.

"Of course, you can stay, Marie," the nun said as she turned toward Angela. "She seems to be fascinated with the altar protectors. Here is a brochure on the gargoyles."

"Do not touch anything," said Angela. "We'll keep the door to Mother's office open."

Angela followed the Mother Superior out of the room.

Marie moved closer to the altar. The dragon gargoyle leaning over the altar was solidly grounded on the table. His energy signaled to keep your distance but also that he was at your service. He was keeping a sharp eye on all activity. The gargoyle with the wings was more relaxed and contemplative; he stepped back and observed. She realized why the Mother Superior chose the two gargoyles. You need active and passive presences in life and in art. The Mother Superior took symbolism to the next level, she thought. The placement of the statues was not random. Maybe they were on the outside of churches to protect those who entered deep contemplation. The gargoyles seemed active to Marie, as active as her experiences inside the mirror.

Marie could hear the two women talking. She moved closer to the open door and leaned in.

"I will need to have several vestments made for Easter Service, along with an altar linen."

"That will not be a problem, Mother."

"How are things with you since Franco passed away?"

"I am managing. I have my family and we are busy. Franco would be proud of this new generation. Thank you for your concern."

Marie had not thought about how Angela was doing since Franco passed. She benefited from Angela's attention but hadn't considered that she might still be grieving.

"Marie is quite the young lady now."

"Yes, she will exceed my expectations, I am sure. She is interested in history."

"I see that she has your spirit and determination."

Marie was concerned about meeting her aunt's expectations. She was going to college, but she wanted to have fun while doing it and to choose a major that interested her. Her dream was to live in Manhattan, and if she had to go to college to accomplish that, then so be it.

"Are you ready?" asked Angela. "We don't want to keep the Mother Superior; she is a busy woman."

"I am ready. Aunt Angela, we need to get you a few gargoyles for your altar. They're useful to have around."

"I do not need a gargoyle," said Angela. "Hurry up, we need to get home. I have a client coming soon."

Angela and Marie descended St. Mary's steep hill.

"Aunt Angela, I am sorry if I have been self-absorbed."

"What do you mean?"

"I know it's been a while since he passed, but you still must be sad about Uncle Franco. We should all be more supportive so you feel comfortable talking about him. You have done so much for us."

"Marie, I have made great compromises in my life, and now I do not have to. Your uncle got me to America so I could have a better life and raise several generations. So, I feel lucky to have met him, but he was not the easiest man to live with. There were things I did not like about my life here, but you and your brothers and sister are not among them."

Angela readied her sewing space for her afternoon client. During the day, the house was quiet, but she was unable to focus all her energy on creating. Mother Superior's choice of adornments for her altar had piqued Angela's interest. Even though Sister Anna Claire was an Episcopal nun, the thought of such pagan symbols seemed more than out of place, but Angela thought maybe there was something to them. Most medieval churches had these creatures built into the outside of their churches, so they were not entirely pagan or evil.

Angela waited for Mrs. Henry Hubbard, who had called Angela weeks ago and made an appointment to see Angela upon her return from Paris. She sounded like a modern enthusiastic woman, well-traveled and educated.

"It's so nice to meet you," said Mrs. Hubbard, as she stepped forward and shook Angela's hand. She had clear skin with the hint of lines around her eyes. Angela surmised she was a woman of about fifty.

"I have heard that you are a wizard when it comes to sewing," said Mrs. Hubbard. "They even say that you transform people with your clothes."

"I am sure that my clients are exaggerating," said Angela. Accolades made Angela uncomfortable; after all, she had been sewing professionally for fifty years and it brought her so much satisfaction that compliments were unnecessary.

"I have seen your work, so I am sure I'm not."

"Did you enjoy Paris?" asked Angela, changing the subject. "I was there many years ago with my husband."

"Yes, my mother was French. She emigrated from Paris during the first World War. I was born here, but I visit my cousins in Paris every few years."

Angela envied Mrs. Hubbard's connection to her family in Europe, wishing that she had a cousin or aunt left in Sicily to connect her with her old life. I am an old woman now, Angela thought. They would all be dead anyway. Angela thought about possible alternative timelines of her life. If the earthquake had not happened, she would have stayed in Sicily and she would not have experienced America's growth through the decades. In essence, she got to rewrite her family history.

"What do you do for work?" Angela asked.

"I am an interior decorator," said Mrs. Hubbard. "I see that we are kindred spirits." She looked around Angela's hallway. "You have a flair."

"Thank you," said Angela. "Are you a native of Nelson-ville?"

"I was raised in New York City. We have an apartment there and a home here in Nelsonville. We have been spending more time in Nelsonville lately. The city is getting so crowd-ed."

"My nephew lives in New York on East 57th Street, and he says the same thing. Is there something special you'd like me to make for you?"

"Well, I was hoping you could make a dress for me. I found this pattern in Paris."

Angela looked at the pattern. The dress was a sleeveless silhouette, and the hemline flared out at the bottom just below the knee; simple and elegant. Delightfully French.

"This is a wonderful design," said Angela.

"My feeling as well. I hope I am not offending you. I know you make your own patterns."

"Not at all. I wish women would choose a look like this more often. You have more variety when it comes to jewelry and color. I think it would look beautiful on you in a shocking pink, with your slim figure and light skin, and you already move with confidence. This will make you appear even more confidant."

"Then shocking pink it is. I would like a light cotton material."

"I will take your measurements, then come by next week and I'll have the material."

Mrs. Hubbard noticed the brochure on the gargoyles that Mother Superior had given Marie. "Is that brochure about the gargoyles on Notre Dame?" she asked.

"Yes, my niece must have forgotten it. She is always leaving things around. They are grotesque images."

"Funny, everyone has a different reaction to gargoyles. Some of my clients request them for their homes."

"For their homes?"

"It is a matter of taste," said Mrs. Hubbard. "Some people see them as purely decorative and others recognize their metaphysical meaning, such as protection and presenting a physical aspect of Hell. Like many symbols of the Old World, they have a multitude of meanings."

"I suppose so," said Angela. She had no idea that so many people knew about gargoyles. They seemed to be hidden until one was ready to see them.

"They do add a focal point to a room, and they certainly inspire conversation," said Mrs. Hubbard. "Some say they remind humans of their connection to the cosmos; that there are other beings in the universe."

"My niece was fascinated by them," said Angela. "You seem to know a lot about them."

"I like to research the pieces I purchase for my clients, and I like to inform my clients about the pieces. It adds meaning to a home design."

"I know a bit about symbolism. I like to keep images of the Blessed Mother around because they have meaning."

"It reminds us of our values and beliefs," said Mrs. Hubbard. "They are extensions of ourselves."

Angela had not thought about symbols or images as an extension of herself. She saw them as separate and to be revered and feared. The Catholic Church taught that one should fear God, but the truth was that Angela did not fear God—she feared losing people.

"I will see you next week," said Angela. An interesting conversation, she mused.

After Mrs. Hubbard left, Angela perused the brochure. The idea of the gargoyles protecting spaces was intriguing. She turned off the light and went to prepare supper before Felicia and the children arrived home.

Chapter 5

Beginning Again
December 1969

For eight months, Robert worked for a tile design company and rented a house with friends in Nelsonville with land to clandestinely grow and sell marijuana. He had learned construction and design from Franco, and he was now putting it to use.

Robert sat at the kitchen table on Morning Glory Avenue, where there was the usual chatter and activity in the house but with a lighter energy in the air. During the Christmas season, the house took on a glow and sense of anticipation. Angela burned apple skins on the stove for a rich aroma, and red candles were peppered throughout the dining room and hallway.

"Robert," said Angela, "you have your own house now, so I want to give you a little money for Christmas." She put a roll of bills in his shirt pocket and hugged him.

"Thank you, Aunt Angela," said Robert. "But I have a good business and now I have a job, and they're training me."

"I still want to help you and contribute," said Angela.

"Angela, are you ready to go shopping?" asked Felicia as she came down the back stairs. "Why are you giving him money?"

"Just a few dollars to get him started," said Angela. "Felicia, I hope you do not mind. He is working so hard."

Felicia knew about her son's marijuana business. He had started selling weed in high school, and she had hoped that he would acquire business acumen and move on into a legitimate business venture. She disapproved of Angela's handouts but realized growing up without a father had not been easy.

"Okay," said Felicia, resigned. "I know that you mean well, but we should not make this a habit. You need your money."

"Thanks, Aunt Angela," said Robert. "I'll put it to good use."

"You need to be careful with that business of yours," said Felicia. "What if you get arrested?"

"The police are my friends," said Robert.

"So you think," said Felicia. "You should concentrate on tile design and maybe start your own business someday."

"I'm thinking about it." Robert leaned back in his chair.

"Your Uncle Franco had his own business and so can you," said Angela.

"Yes, but first establish yourself with your present job and learn the ropes," said Felicia. "That is the best strategy. Don't you agree, Angela?"

Angela believed in strategy, but sometimes you had to jump in and see where life took you. She knew that stability was important to Felicia, but one could also create stability by taking chances.

"Generally, I would agree; but if Robert feels he has the skills to start a business, maybe it is worth a try."

"Really, Angela, why are you contradicting me? I have enough things to worry about."

"It is best for Robert to make his own decisions."

"And who will pick up the pieces when he goes bankrupt? I don't agree with giving out money for failures, but you do."

"I'm sitting right here," interjected Robert. "I will start my business when I'm ready."

Angela and Felicia looked at one another and remained silent for a moment.

"All right," said Felicia. "I agree with that."

Angela nodded.

The next week, Mrs. Hubbard returned for her fitting. She began talking the minute Angela opened the door.

"Hello, Angela, I hope you don't mind, but I had a few items in my storage that might interest you." She placed her bag on the floor and pulled out two lion statues. "These are replicas of what are on top of the bell tower of the Messina Cathedral. They function similarly to the gargoyles. You will be reminded that your house is protected, but with images from Sicily."

Angela knew the Messina Cathedral was built in the 12th century but destroyed in the earthquakes in 1783 and 1908 and again in a two-day fire from a bomb during World War II. Each time it had been rebuilt. She recalled a letter she had received from the Mother Superior in Palermo, saying that the cathedral had experienced a fire from a bombing.

"Much of the cathedral was destroyed during the earthquake in 1908," said Angela. "I remembered walking through the area afterward."

"Oh, I am so sorry you experienced that. I hope I didn't bring up awful memories."

"No, that is fine. I was visiting Sicily in 1929 and saw it restored, but I haven't seen it since the war."

"It has the largest astronomical clock in the world," said Mrs. Hubbard. "It is quite beautiful to see."

"You have been to Messina?"

"Yes, a few years ago my husband, who is an historian and teaches at Columbia University, and I toured southern Italy. The highlight was the astronomical clock in the campanile at the cathedral. We went up into the tower for a spectacular view of the city."

"What kind of clock is that?"

"An astronomical clock has moving parts that tell us the position of the sun, moon, zodiacal constellations and major planets. It was added in 1933 to mark the rebuilding after the earthquake. That is how I understand it. The lions are a symbol of strength."

"Thank you so much," said Angela as she picked up the statues. "They are beautiful."

"I hope you don't think I'm forward in bringing them," said Mrs. Hubbard. "Amazing, it had been destroyed so many times but rebuilt. Now that is a testament to perseverance. A falling tower moment does not have to be the end. I am sure you know that firsthand. Now let's get to my fitting."

Everyone has the experience of hitting bottom, but Angela had transformed what could have been a life full of stagnation and regret into an expansive experience that reached into the unseen world. She reflected on the recent appearance of gargoyles and lion statues in her life. The only images she had on her fireplace mantles, hanging art reproductions, and altar were standard Catholic images, but she felt lately that things were shifting. Time moves on, she thought, and everything changes. Angela was not nostalgic for the past. The gargoyles and lions were from the past, but they represented something different in the present. Maybe they represented a new beginning of strength, which Angela fully embraced. A new decade was approaching, and Angela braced herself for more changes.

"Thank you. I will put one in my bedroom and the other on the hallway mantle."

"This is excellent. You will have protection when you sleep and from people with negative energy who might come into your home."

After Mrs. Hubbard left, Angela placed one of the lions on her mantle. The animal projected a fierce determination to protect the environment in which it was placed.

"Where did you get the lion?" Marie asked, flopping on a chair. She wore a French braid that extend to her mid-back.

"My client brought them. They are replicas of the lions on top of Messina Cathedral. They are a symbol of protection like the gargoyles. She is an interior designer. I can't believe that people hire someone else to decorate their home."

"How perfect," said Marie. "Your hometown is protecting you."

"I suppose it is. Maybe we never really leave our birth-place."

"Hi, Lizzy," said Marie.

"*Ciao, bella,*" said Lizzy.

"Get a cup and saucer from the pantry," said Angela.

Marie was dressed in a green wool mini-skirt Angela had made, along with a white top. It took many discussions between Marie and Angela to put the hem that far above the knee.

"You are going to be cold in that short skirt," said Angela.

"I have tights on," said Marie. "I got this letter today from City College," she squealed, waving a letter. She handed the letter to Angela as she twirled around the kitchen.

"You have been accepted to City College, and you start next September. I am so happy." Angela hugged Marie. Angela's dream had finally come true.

"It's early acceptance so now I can do other things here, besides going to class," said Marie. "Like spend time with you ladies. What are you talking about?" asked Marie. "Can I have some coffee?"

Marie knew that her good news would spread like a wildfire as soon as Angela could get to a phone.

Angela was pleased that Marie could go out in the world and get an education, but she did not like the way Marie dressed. Angela did not understand why everyone wanted to look slovenly. In Sicily, if people dressed in blouses that hung over baggy pants it was assumed that they were of the lower classes. At this time, in America it was considered chic.

"She has such a cute figure," said Lizzy.

"I think the hem is too short," said Angela.

"That's the rage now," said Lizzy. "If I had a cute figure and good legs, I'd wear a mini skirt."

"Marie, you better go to school this afternoon," said Angela. "Your mother has enough to deal with. She does not

need the school calling about your truancy. And your acceptance letter says you must graduate from high school. You
need to call her at the office about your acceptance."

"They won't even notice I'm not there," said Marie. "But
I'll go this afternoon, and I'll tell mom when she gets home."

Marie enjoyed going into the city a few times a month on
school days. She had intentionally kept a low profile at school
so she would not be terribly missed. Her friends might notice
but not enough to inquire about her absence. The grittiness of
Times Square appealed to her. One could get lost in the mass of
humanity that called 42nd Street home in the 1960s. Soon, she
would call Manhattan home.

"Call her now," said Angela. "She would want to know."

"Time for me to go," said Lizzy. "Congratulations, Marie.
Your aunt has been talking about you going to college for
years."

"Thanks, Lizzy."

Marie dialed her mother's office.

"Mom, I got into City College in Manhattan; early
acceptance."

She heard a pause on the other end and a sigh.

"What will you study? It should be something useful."

"I'll just have to see," said Marie. She had learned to be
diplomatic when it came to her mother. It gave her mom a
sense of doing her motherly duty to make sure that her
children's future would be secure. It was best to placate and fall
into the background.

"I don't know yet. I just want to live in New York and
study. Maybe I'll be an urban gypsy."

"You need to have a marketable skill. I think you have
done too much daydreaming."

"It was a joke. I'll think about a practical major."

Marie never discussed her experiences with the unseen
world with her mother. It was something that she shared with
Angela, and Marie was starting to suspect that her connection
to the invisible world prove to be invaluable. She found her

mother's suspicion for anything intangible exasperating, so she decided to throw caution to the wind.

"I think the Liberal Arts program would suit me," said Marie. She knew this would displease Felicia to no end.

"Liberal Arts? What kind of job do you hope to get?"

"See you when you get home."

"Did you tell your mother?" asked Angela.

"Yes, and I think it made her really excited."

That night, Angela thanked the universe and the Blessed Mother for putting Marie on the right path—or better yet, the path she had set for Marie. She had less than a year of Marie under her roof before she would leave for college.

Chapter 6
NEW YEAR'S EVE, 1969
EMERGING

The world was on the threshold of a new decade, and Angela prepared for New Year's dinner. Snow was lightly falling, blanketing the ground, and winter was taking hold. The Vietnam War still raged, but it affected her family less since Robert was home and Frank was still in college. She sensed that this would be a new decade of immense change. When she thought of her unseen friends, they confirmed her suspicions.

She thought about the choices she had made over the years and how she had made them in partnership with her unseen friends. They were never far from her mind, and lately she felt there was less of a delineation between herself and these energies. Angela thought about the night ahead, celebrating the coming year and all that it would bring. Angela looked up at the lion statue on the mantle and smiled. You will be protecting my family, thought Angela, and I am grateful.

Angela and Felicia put the green lentils, pork, tortellini, and thick crust pizza in serving dishes. Frank, Andrea, Marie, and Robert sat at the table. As they were placing the dishes on the white tablecloth, Angela paused and looked at everyone gathered around her and smiled.

"Good wishes for the New Year," she said. She lifted a bottle of Martini & Rossi Asti Spumante and poured everyone a glass.

"Great—alcohol," said Andrea.

"Yeah, we'd like to see you drunk," said Robert.

"No one gets drunk here," said Angela. "No one makes a *brutta figura* at the dinner table."

The family toasted to a happy and fruitful new year. They were a new American family, immigrant and first- and second-generation Americans all together. It was not an easy journey for Angela to create the family she wanted, but she felt it finally happened. Her legacy would live on long after she passed into spirit.

Angela thought that she had Franco to thank for her good fortune. Without him, the family she saw in front of her would not exist, and because of this she missed him. It was challenging for her to keep up with the new generation, and it required a great deal of energy. Some of her friends from the old days had died, and she missed the familiarity of easy conversation.

"Let's eat," said Andrea. "I want some pizza."

Frank and Robert each lit cigarettes.

"Put those out," said Felicia. "We haven't started eating yet. How can you eat and smoke?"

"Easy," said Frank.

"I have made pork sausage with green lentils. In Italy it is considered good luck for the New Year, and the lentils are in the shape of coins—so it brings prosperity. It will melt in your mouth."

Large round patties of pork sat on top of green lentils.

"What about the pizza?" asked Andrea.

"The pizza is just my regular pizza," said Angela.

"It's yummy," said Marie.

Both boys snuffed out their cigarettes and filled their plates.

"I got a card from Uncle Joe today from Puerto Vallarta, Mexico, wishing us a Happy New Year," said Angela. "He will be back soon and will visit us next weekend."

"Great," said Marie. "It's always fun to see him. I'm hoping he can stay overnight."

"I will suggest it. Sadie and Lizzy are coming by for dessert tonight," Angela told them.

The family ate and talked about the possibilities presented by the new year ahead.

"I think fashion merchandising is a good way for me to go and have my own boutique someday," said Andrea.

"That is an achievable goal," said Felicia.

"I think it's possible that I could start my own tile design business this year," said Robert. "I've learned a lot."

"That is certainly good to hear," said Felicia, as she turned her attention toward Marie. "What about you, Marie?" asked Felicia. "You should take your cues from your brother and study something practical in college."

"I think studying history is practical. This way you don't make the same mistake twice. Anyway, I will have a lot of choices once I get to college."

"Technology is beginning to take off, and it will change how we communicate," said Frank. "I think it's possible for me to get a job in New York designing computer systems in the future and be part of that transformation. I still have my 2-S deferment, but I might have to go into the Reserves once I graduate."

"What about you, Aunt Angela?" Marie asked. "What do you hope for in the new year?

"What I have right here," said Angela. "All of you doing well and happy."

"I can't argue with that," said Felicia. "I hope for the same thing."

In all, the conversation was positive in laying the groundwork for the time ahead. Once the table was cleared, Angela made coffee.

"Here we are," said Lizzy, letting a burst of cold air in. "Hope we're not late."

"Come in. "We're just putting out the dessert," said Felicia as she placed tiramisu and zeppole on the table.

"Coffee?" offered Angela.

"Hi, Angie," said Sadie. "It's cold out there." She took off her coat and gloves and rubbed her hands together.

"Hi all," said Lizzy. "Happy New Year." She handed Angela a bottle of *prosecco*.

"Thank you, Lizzy," said Angela.

"That's from both of us," said Sadie. "Happy New Year, everyone. Let's open it."

"This bottle is for our hostess—not just for you," said Lizzy.

"That's right," said Sadie. She reached into her bag and pulled out another bottle of prosecco and placed it in front of her. "This one is for me."

Everyone laughed.

"How are you, Sadie, Lizzy?" asked Frank.

"We're both fine," said Sadie.

"Speak for yourself," said Lizzy. "My doctor wants me to lose weight because my heart is skipping beats. Doctors—what do they know?"

Angela felt herself to be wealthy with good friends and family. For the first time in her life, she felt completely safe. She did not feel compelled to measure her speech or chastise herself for her thoughts. When Franco was alive, it was about his conversation and how he wanted to express himself. She never thought she could do the same.

Experiencing this new generation was profoundly enlightening. They were birthing a new perspective into the world. New ideas did not flourish when Angela was young, especially if those ideas came from a woman. This generation emerging into adulthood would change the world for the better. Like a crab that has outgrown its shell, the next generation was expanding their boundaries. She felt she had done her job well in supporting that growth. "We already had our toast to the new year, but we can have another before we have dessert," said Angela.

"Open the *prosecco*," said Sadie.

"I'm with you, Sadie," said Marie. "I love the bubbles."

Felicia poured the *prosecco*, and everyone raised their glasses.

"Here's to Peace on Earth," said Angela. Angela was eager to experience the next decade and all the changes waiting in the wings.

"So, Marie," Sadie said. "You'll be graduating high school in June, and I hear you'll be going to college in New York City."

"I can't wait," Marie said as she sipped her prosecco. "I am so happy I'll be living in New York. The possibilities are endless. I'll be staying at the YWCA until I find a roommate and get an apartment."

"They're endless if you have money," said Felicia. "You will have to focus."

"Felicia, way to take wind out of someone's sails," said Sadie.

"I'm just being practical, and I don't want her to make the mistake of getting an education without the possibility of employment."

"She should do what interests her," said Angela.

"Sure, as long as it is practical. Where would I be if I did not have a business background? Keep that in mind."

"Robert gets handsomer every day," Lizzy said, diffusing the tension. "He's got that curly black hair and a Roman nose."

"He's such a pothead," said Andrea. "He'll end up in jail someday."

"Don't say that," said Angela nonchalantly. "Nobody is going to jail. He has a job, and I'm sure he'll have his own business someday. I know people who work in construction; I could give them a call." Over the years Angela and Franco had helped many people, and they owed her favors she would not be shy about collecting.

"Well, I have a date," said Frank.

"Oh," said Sadie. "Who is the lucky girl?"

"Is she local?" asked Lizzy. "We might know her."

"Frank is dating Judge Lowenstein's daughter," said Robert. "Lucky for me if I run into trouble with my business. I'll take my dessert and go upstairs and relax," said Robert.

"You mean you're going to smoke a joint," said Andrea.

"Mind your business," said Robert. "I'll take some dessert with me."

"A judge's daughter. That is a fine match," said Sadie.

"Oh yes, very fine," said Lizzy.

"Frank, what is your date's name?" asked Sadie.

"Sarah, but it's not serious," Frank said. "We're casually dating."

"You're young and should play the field. What do you think, Felicia?" asked Lizzy.

"I think he should do what he wants," said Felicia.

"By any standard, it is a good match," said Sadie.

"You old ladies should stop trying to set people up," said Angela. "Why are you so interested in people dating? Why don't you two get new husbands?"

"I don't want a husband," said Sadie. "I'm playing the field like Frank, only with old men who don't know what day it is."

Felicia was sipping her wine and tried to stifle a laugh, but the wine sprayed everywhere. Everyone laughed at the thought of Sadie serially dating old men.

"What? You don't believe me? Love them and leave them—that's what I say. Marie, look for men with one foot in the grave. That way you get everything."

The laughter resounded throughout the dining room.

"You are a rascal, Sadie," said Angela. "Your poor dead husbands. How did they live with you?"

"Very well, Angela. I took care of them, and they were grateful. Let us raise a glass to my deceased husbands; may they rest in peace."

"I never knew your husbands," said Marie, "but I'm sure I would have liked them."

"Two were pretty likable but the last one wasn't," said Sadie. "He was a cheap bastard."

Marie had noticed that within the Italian-American immigrant community, when the husband died the wives then lived fuller lives. She did not notice heart-wrenching grief, just an acceptance of the inevitability of death. The women never railed against death, and in some cases they thanked death for releasing them from a marriage that had been on life support for years.

"What about you, Lizzy?" asked Marie. "Do you miss your husband?"

"Sure, I miss him, honey," said Lizzy. "He was reliable like a comfortable chair and he always brought home a paycheck. My mother was right; it was a good match."

"Wow," said Robert as he put his dessert on a plate. "He was like an old chair. Lucky you didn't put him out with the trash."

"There were times I wanted to," laughed Lizzy.

"Let's toast to Lizzy's husband," said Marie.

"This is the last toast," said Angela. "I'm going to make coffee."

Everyone raised their glasses.

"To Lizzy's husband, who is with God," said Angela, "and to the New Year, not far away. May we all prosper and receive blessings for the next decade."

They all drank as Frank said his goodbyes and went off to meet the judge's daughter. Sadie and Lizzy declined the coffee and put on their coats while Felicia cleared the table. Angela felt it was an auspicious beginning to the new year and that the days ahead would hold many unexpected events—some good, some challenging, but all of it an opportunity to express herself and be victorious.

Angela walked her guests to the front door.

"What's this?" asked Lizzy. She noticed the brochure on the Notre Dame gargoyles on the hall table.

"I got that from the Mother Superior at St. Mary's School," said Angela. She did not want to elaborate on her experience at the school.

"Ooh, some of them are so ugly," said Lizzy.

"Let me see," said Sadie. She perused the brochure. "One of them looks like my last husband."

"Maybe he's a relation," said Lizzy.

"Okay, *le signore*, have a safe walk home," said Angela.

"Why the rush?" asked Lizzy. "Do you have a date?"

The guests laughed as they exited the house. Angela waved to them from the window as they descended the porch stairs. In her preparation for tonight's dinner, Angela had questioned her unseen friends about whether she should just have the family at the table or invite guests. They made it clear that she needed to have other influences at her New Year's Eve dinner. She was told that the beginning of a decade was an important event that should be shared with others, so Angela had invited the least formal of her friends.

"Are you making coffee, Aunt Angela?" asked Marie.

"I think it is too late for coffee," said Angela.

"I want to stay up until midnight."

"I will make a small amount for just you and me. I think your mother is tired."

The aroma of the espresso brewing on the stove permeated the kitchen. Marie had smelled the strong coffee brewing in the morning ever since she could remember. It suggested the beginning of a day with all its possibilities. Now it suggested the new year and a myriad of potential realities.

"I like Sadie and Lizzy," said Marie. "They are funny ladies." Angela washed the dishes as Marie dried.

"You only see one side of them," Angela said. "They had a hard time growing up, and yet they have kept their sense of humor through it all."

"What happened to them growing up?"

"They were poor, and their fathers were mean people. There was no one to protect them. They married men with a little money, and now they are both comfortable widows. You never know what people have been through."

"I'm sorry to hear that. They're such good ladies."

"You should not be sorry. Now they are strong and independent and live their lives the way they want. If they did not have those experiences, they would not be who they are. Like me."

"What do you mean?"

"If I had not experienced the earthquake, I would not be here—and that would be a tragedy."

"Maybe you were fated to be here with us."

"Maybe, but remember, the face people show you is only a portion of who they really are."

The dishes put away, Marie and Angela sat in stillness as the dining room clock chimed midnight.

"It is 1970. Happy New Year, Aunt Angela."

Angela was eager to experience the next decade and all the changes waiting in the wings.

Chapter 7
Transformation

Spring peeked out through the blossoming trees in the backyard of Morning Glory Avenue as Angela brought her houseplants out to enjoy the sun. The light was returning, and a feeling of renewal was in the air. Blooming honeysuckle wrapped around the entrance to the backyard. It was a warm, glorious day in Nelsonville. She sat in a reclining chair on the side porch, closed her eyes, and offered her face to the sun. She remembered that spring was a special time in Sicily.

"A few more months and I will graduate," said Marie, coming at the door. "Oh, I'm sorry, were you taking a nap?"

"No, I was thinking about spring in Sicily. It was a time when my father would return from the silk trade in the Middle East and my mother would prepare an elaborate meal."

"You have never talked about him. What was he like?"

Angela loved Marie's curiosity about times past. It was not something young people thought much about. They seemed to care only for the moment.

"He was a silk trader and handsome with dark, wavy hair and kind eyes that sparkled when the sun hit them. One day we had received word that my father was on his way home and would reach Messina in a week. My mother began to prepare for his return. He was journeying through the overland silk trade road, which was fraught with treacherous terrain and bandits."

"Bandits? That must have been dangerous."

"It was, but he made good money. After two weeks, he still had not returned. My mother was frantic. She found a group of merchants who had traveled with my father. They were disheveled and exhausted. They had been robbed along the route, and they told her my father had been killed. The rest of the traders got away, but they were not able to retrieve his body. My mother buried an empty coffin."

"That must have been awful," Marie said.

"It was for my mother. He was traveling a lot when I was a child, so my memory of him is vague."

Angela had not thought of her father in years. When she was young, she wondered what happened to his body. Did the birds devour him, or did some kind soul dig a grave so he could go to his rest? She never knew if her sister had survived the earthquake or if her father had found a resting place, so she had learned to embrace the uncertainty of life and carry on. Her unseen friends often applauded her choice to move ahead, regardless of the situation.

"I'm glad you told me about him. That just expands my perception of who you are. I'm going to the store; do you want to come?"

"No, I am going to rest here and enjoy May."

Angela's thoughts drifted and focused inward, expanding into her inner landscape. There were hills and valleys of feelings, thoughts, and images. She settled on top of a mountain looking down at what seemed to be her history on earth. She gazed below and focused on a brick wall. She saw herself telling a man that this was the last place her sister had been seen and pulling out a photograph of a young, unkempt girl with fearful eyes standing in front of the wall. Deep circles were embedded under the girl's eyes, and the radiating fear in her eyes was combined with hopelessness.

"See," the visionary said to what seemed to be the authorities. "This is where she was last seen. You need to look here. You need to find her. Find who took this picture."

Angela felt she was drifting deeper, and images came streaming by her without sense or reason. She felt she was flying through time, past this lifetime and beyond space that only those with open hearts and minds could access. The space felt infinite, devoid of linear time. It was the well of possibility—a formless place that could be molded into form. She slowed and drifted past people she knew she had loved, but they were not from this lifetime. Angela saw that she had other connections in times past who had shaped who she was in the present and who she would be in the future. "Every experience is designed to teach, so the soul becomes stronger and more resilient," she had been told by one of her unseen friends who was now present in her vision. She now saw that this disappointment, or that joy, was but fleeting on a vast landscape without boundaries.

"Aunt Angela," said Marie, coming up the steps. "Do you have any rolls? I just bought some jam."

She waited for Angela to respond, but her aunt did not move. A wave of anxiety washed over Marie. She gingerly approached Angela. She had never seen her aunt so still.

"Aunt Angela, are you alright?" She took measured steps to see if she was breathing. She placed her hand on Angela's arm, and she opened her eyes.

"Were you sleeping?" asked Marie.

"I don't know," said Angela. She shook her head and rubbed her hands together. "I'm not sure, but think I was dreaming. It was a strange dream. It was as if I was visiting places."

"Do you have any rolls in the oven? I heard your timer go off."

"Yes, let us go inside."

"You looked like you were far away," said Marie.

"I was remembering."

"Remembering what?"

"Something that happened a long time ago," said Angela. "I think I saw a photograph of my sister, and I stood in front of a stone wall—the kind you would find in Sicily—and I told the people who were looking for this older version of her to start at the wall because she was there."

"How do you know it was your sister? You didn't find her when you returned to Sicily."

"It just came to my mind when I woke up that it was her."

"Maybe she's trying to communicate with you," said Marie. "But I'm sure she died in the earthquake. How could she have survived?"

Angela wondered why she had been shown her life on earth. She thought that was reserved for her physical death when God judged her, but it seemed that anyone could observe their deeds in this lifetime and change their ways.

"Sounds like what I saw at Bryant Park when I closed my eyes and drifted. Really felt like traveling through time."

"Maybe." Angela never thought about time travel within her mind, but it resonated.

"I think I'll go to school today," said Marie.

"Why today?" asked Angela. She took the rolls out of the oven and placed them in a basket with pats of butter.

"I just think it would be good to show up. It's amazing, but this semester I never attended gym class once, and I've passed."

"I don't see why that is important," said Angela.

"Exactly," said Marie. "I'm glad you see it that way. It is so boring. I would rather go horseback riding. That is exercise. What are you doing today?"

"I have two clients," said Angela, massaging her fingers. "I'm beginning to have arthritis in my hands."

Marie saw that her aunt's knuckles were protruding from the bone and had become less nimble. She hoped that Angela would be able to continue her craft for a few more years. Marie knew how important it was to her aunt.

"I should take some aspirin," said Angela.

"Move your hands around, Aunt Angela," said Marie. "That will help." Ever since Marie could remember, her aunt seemed old. But now with the changes in her fingers, Marie saw the results of aging, and that made her see her aunt as mortal. She recognized that one day Angela would no longer be baking bread or sewing. She would pass into the infinite space when she died.

"I would miss you if you weren't here," said Marie.

"You will be busy creating your own life, but if you think of me now and then I would be happy. Now, go on to school," said Angela. "Grace them with your presence. You only have a few more weeks left."

"You're right, and then it is summer!"

Marie picked up her roll and ate it as she left the house.

"Where are your books?" called Angela.

"In my locker, where they've been all year."

Marie reminded Angela of her sister-in-law, Speranza, Marie's grandmother, who had to suppress the independent, confident part of herself to conform to what society found acceptable for a woman. This generation of Italian-Americans, especially Marie, would not be concerned with conforming or care about what someone else thought about her choices. The 1970s were about evolving past the generation that was raised by Italian immigrants, not just materially but intellectually and creatively. The new decade would be a harbinger of change.

Angela went into the dining room and began to cut out a dress pattern. She thought again about the frightened girl in the photograph. She remembered there was a sense of familiarity with the tattered garment the girl wore. Angela stopped cutting the pattern and stared at the oval mirror that hung on the dining room wall. Time had not existed in her vision, but it came to an abrupt stop now, and she heard her unseen friends. The garment the girl wore was the nightgown Angela wore the morning of the earthquake. She realized she was being shown a version of herself, not her sister, if she had made the choice to stay in Sicily with the nuns. Angela was shown that she might have ended up as a missing person who authorities would have had little interest in finding.

She surveyed her dining room and all that she had created and felt she could embrace the 1970s and all the changes the new decade would bring.

It was a warm, late-summer day, and it was time for Marie to leave for college. Her mother and brother, Frank, would accompany her to the city. Angela stood at the front door and made sure that Marie was appropriately dressed to step into her new life. For Marie, it was a sad moment that she was leaving Angela, but she was happy to leave the small-town life of Nelsonville. She had often felt she was marking time, and now she was feeling movement in her life.

"You look happy," said Angela. "I hope you will think of us occasionally and come home some weekends. You are just a short train ride away."

"Sure, Aunt Angela," said Marie. "Thank you for the new skirt and blouse."

"It makes an impression when you meet new people," said Angela. "Remember to visit your Uncle Joe when you can."

Angela put her hand on Marie's shoulder, and then she touched her cheek.

"I will miss you," said Angela. "Everything I am, I hope I have given to you."

"Is everything in the car?" asked Frank. "Let's get going. Mom's already in the car, and after I drop you off, I have a meeting in the city."

"I'm ready," said Marie. "Aunt Angela, I want you to know that I appreciate everything you have taught me. I know I will use my intuition and connection to the unseen world. If I have any problems, I know where to find you."

Angela walked with Marie on the front porch and watched as the family drove away. She reflected on how it was so different from the time her nephew Joe left the confines of Nelsonville almost three decades ago. She and Franco had walked Joe to the train station and Joe had set out on his own. She had cried because she felt he was alone and there was no one to accompany him to his new life once he arrived in New York City. Now, Marie was accompanied by her family to her new life and would have support with this transition, so there was no need for her to go to the station. Angela hoped that she had had an influence in this positive outcome.

Angela's great-nieces and -nephews had left the house one by one to start their lives, so the noise level had gradually declined. Like a play, each character was leaving the stage until only the main character was left.

Angela remembered how her influence had penetrated Marie's awareness when Felicia and the children had spent the summer of 1959 at Felicia's parents' home in Cohasset, Massachusetts a year after Nunzio had died. Marie, age seven, had called Angela from Cohasset.

"Aunt Angela," said Marie. "This is Marie. How are you? I miss you."

"Marie, how nice to hear from you. I miss you too. Everything is okay here. I will be glad when you come home."

"Me too," said Marie.

"Are you having a good summer?" Angela asked.

"Yes, we go to the beach all the time. We're having fun."

"We should not talk too long because it will cost too much."

"Will you make clothes for me when I get back?"

"Of course, you know I will. I am taking care of your Uncle Franco, so I will fill my days until you return."

"I miss your stories and talking with you, Aunt Angela."

"We will see each other soon," said Angela. "When you get back, we will have a pizza party and I will measure you for new outfits. I am sure you will grow over the summer. Enjoy your time by the sea, and play with the other children. When you are on the beach, think of me."

"I do think of you all the time." Angela's heart was warmed by that phone call from a seven-year-old. It got her through the summer.

That year, Felicia and the children arrived back in Nelsonville just before Labor Day. As soon they pulled in the driveway, Angela ran to the car and embraced Felicia and the children.

"I have missed you all so much. It has been a long summer without you."

When her family left for Felicia's summer house, Angela disliked the quiet even though she was often surly about how much noise the children made. Franco spent his days in the basement workshop or in the garden, making the house feel even emptier.

Angela had settled into the next phase of her life after Marie left for college. There were several deaths within the Italian-American community, so their cultural influence was diminishing. She was sad that friends were dying, but the progressive ideas that were taking over the new decade interested her. Marie was coming home from college for her first weekend visit, and Angela had prepared a pizza.

"Here I am," called Marie as she opened the front door. "Aunt Angela, are you around?"

"You're early," said Angela. She wiped her hands on a dishtowel and opened her arms. "Did your mother pick you up at the station?"

"Yeah, she dropped me off and went back to the office. My professor let us out early. I've missed you. I'm glad we have this time alone."

"I have coffee on the stove if you would like some. You need to tell me all about college."

They sat at their usual places at the kitchen table. Marie looked out the window at the fall foliage, breathing in the scents of her childhood. The leaves, coated in various shades of oranges, reds, and olive greens, swayed as the fall breeze swept through. She hated to see the warm weather wane. The fall always signaled the end to her time on New England beaches when she was a kid. She loved spring, summer, and fall, but winter was the most unpredictable season, full of frigid temperatures and snow that interrupted life's flow. Everything contracted in winter.

"How is your arthritis?" Marie asked.

"Oh, it is about the same. I take aspirin. I can still sew, but it is more difficult." She poured the coffee. "I have some anisette cookies."

"Thank you, Aunt Angela."

"Do you like college?" asked Angela.

"A lot more than I liked high school," said Marie. "Aunt Angela, do you remember you used to tell us the story of the good and bad angels?"

"Yes, I remember. You and your sister came into my sitting room every night to hear the story. You especially requested the good and bad angel story."

"Where did you get the stories? Did someone tell you?"

"The story was about the fall of Lucifer. Everyone knows the story. He disobeyed God, so he was cast into Hell."

"Yes, but you talked about other angels who disagreed with God, but they weren't cast into Hell. Like Archangel Michael, who threatened God with mutiny if he could not act without God's permission. You also had other spiritual beliefs. Where did they come from?"

"Why are you asking these questions? I told those stories so long ago. Are you having more experiences with mirrors? You know there is a dark side to that."

"I am taking a class in comparative religions and alternative spiritual beliefs, and I thought who better to ask about alternative beliefs? For example, your altar to The Blessed Mother."

"An altar to The Blessed Mother is not an alternative belief," said Angela.

"If you worship and consult Mary before you worship God, it is an alternative way of thinking. There is an entire ancient goddess culture around the sacred feminine."

"Your uncle prayed to Mary years ago to save my life when I was seriously ill. The next day I was sitting up in bed, so I created an altar to The Virgin, and I still light candles every week in thanks. To this day, I am grateful. This is not worship."

"What about necromancy, talking to the dead? That is an alternative belief. Remember, we talked about this, and we've both had visions."

"Necro what?"

"Necromancy. It is the practice of communicating with the dead. It is considered a magical practice, and the class goes into those practices. It is what you have done your whole life."

"You're talking about this in class?"

"Yes, people practice necromancy. Like yourself. The experiences in the mirror are vivid in my mind. I think that is a kind of necromancy. Is it taught or just innate like yours?"

"You should be careful. Remember what I told you about the mirror. I know you are interested in the unseen, but you must control it so it does not control you."

Andrea came in through the side door.

"Hey, Sis, what are you doing here?"

"I'm home for the weekend."

Andrea picked up an anisette cookie.

"Wash your hands first," Angela said.   She turned to Marie. "We can finish this conversation later."

Angela felt that revealing her spiritual beliefs or practices would weaken their power and open her up to more criticism. Over the years, she had dropped enough hints about her inner world so that Marie could cultivate her own relationship with the unseen. She did not want to tell Marie what to believe. She wanted her to find out for herself how to move forward. The idea of alternative spiritual practices was in its infancy, but Angela's unseen friends told her that eventually many people would seek a new spirituality.

When she was at the convent in Palermo, one of the nuns overheard Angela talking to her missing sister, begging her sister to tell her if she was alive or dead.

"You should not contact the dead," said the nun. "To speak to the dead, you must go through God. He will decide if you are worthy of an answer. It is a blasphemy to think you are talking to your sister. It could be the devil."

Angela then hid her beliefs, fearful of the consequences. But it was natural for Angela to communicate with the unseen world, like breathing.

"What are we talking about?" asked Andrea.

"I was just asking your sister about college," said Angela.

"How's it going, sis?"

Marie was not sure how much she should tell her family about her experience so far. Living in New York was exceptional on many levels, but the most enlightening part was meeting people from all over the world. Her life would never be the same. Even if at times it was a struggle, she did not miss living at home. When Marie grew up, there were many influences in the house at Morning Glory Avenue. There had always been a steady stream of at least three generations of her family that came and went at the house on various occasions. Sadie and Lizzy provided comic relief, and Angela's more traditional friends from the Italian-American community gave Marie a sense of tradition. Together with Angela's spirituality and her mother's success in business, it all came together to create an acceptance of who people were. When she ventured off to college, she was able to integrate her new surrounding easier than most.

"I'm doing well," said Marie. "I love living in New York, and I hope to go to grad school."

"You're thinking about that already?" Andrea asked. "You just started college."

"All the girls are thinking about it," said Marie. "Everyone looks ahead."

"That is nice," said Angela. "Always good to think about your future. When your mother gets home, we'll all have dinner together."

Angela wondered what Nunzio would have thought about his daughter attending college. He had not finished high school even though Angela had tried to convince him to. It had been a mammoth effort to wake Nunzio up in the morning to go to school. Sometimes she had to wet a facecloth and press it on his head to get him to move. At least when Marie refused to go to school, it was because she had interests elsewhere. Her father had just slept.

"I think I will major in history," said Marie. "I've always had a connection to historical events and how the world has evolved, and I love storytelling."

"What kind of job will you get?" Andrea asked. "Mom's not going to like that."

"I am sure she will be able to get a job," said Angela.

Marie knew that her mother did not care for Angela's storytelling. Felicia felt it encouraged an air of self-indulgence that was inappropriate for success in the world. Her brother Frank was an electrical engineer, Robert designed and installed tiles, and it was discussed that Andrea would become a retail merchandiser, given her interest in fashion and business. Marie was not interested in following a traditional job path, and Felicia disliked Angela's encouragement.

For dinner that night, Angela made her special pizza and a salad. It was an informal gathering around the dining table where everyone talked at once and there was a feeling of lightness, of homecoming. Angela felt that the years were catching up to her a bit, like the arthritis in her hands and her hips that sometimes bothered her. She had not thought much about aging, but the process had begun. She wanted to keep sewing for as long as she could continue to provide beauty in the world through garments.

She'd revealed to Marie that ever since the earthquake and the tsunami that followed, she had been terrified of thunderstorms. As soon as grey skies and wind rolled in, she would close all the windows and pull the shades. Beads of sweat would appear on her upper lip, and her breathing would become shallow. As she aged, the fear became more forceful, and Angela could not hide from her experience.

"I picked up some wine in the city today," Frank said. He uncorked the bottle of Merlot.

"Let's all have a glass," said Marie.

"Do you know that Marie is going to major in history?" asked Andrea.

"Did you have to say that?" Marie hissed.

"History?" asked Felicia. "Are you going to teach? Teachers don't make much money."

"I figure I can study what I want since it's a city college and it's free to the residents of New York City. I'm a resident now."

"You know, I can't figure you," Felicia said. "That is impractical, and you know it. You could go into the medical profession where you're guaranteed a job, or get a business degree."

Free college added to Marie's independence. Her mother's opinion was inconsequential.

"Keep trying," said Marie. "You'll figure me out."

Felicia wanted to reach across the table to slap her daughter, but a long day at the office quelled her anger.

"We should invite Sadie over; she would love this wine," said Robert.

"Nah, she'll drink it all," said Frank.

Everyone laughed, enjoying the levity that Sadie brought even though she was not there.

"I'm home for the weekend. What shall we do?" asked Marie.

"I have a lot going on with my friends," said Andrea.

"You can come shopping with me," said Felicia.

Perfect, thought Marie, a day drowning in complaints. Felicia disliked browsing but Marie enjoyed the quest of finding the perfect item, whether it be clothing or groceries. Her mother's attitude was more hit and run.

"Sounds like fun," said Marie. "But Aunt Angela, weren't you going to fit me for a new dress?"

"Oh, we can do that when you get back from shopping," Angela said.

"Wonderful," said Marie. "I'm looking forward to shopping with you, Mom."

"Huh," Felicia replied. Sarcasm was not lost on her.

Marie moved the grocery cart along store aisles as her mother plucked items off shelves.

"What do you want to eat tonight?"

"Anything is fine. I don't want you to have to cook," Marie offered.

"If I don't cook, we don't eat."

"Aunt Angela always has food," said Marie. "Has she stopped cooking?"

"You shouldn't rely on your aunt so much now. You need to be more independent. She has spoiled you over the years."

"I could cook for us."

"Really? Have you ever cooked a meal before?"

"No, but someday I'll have to. I might as well practice on my family."

"Experiment on your friends."

Marie said nothing and kept moving the cart along the aisles. She did not want to bring up her choice of a major, but she could tell that her mother had that in the back of her mind by her curt statements.

"I'll make fish like my mother used to make," said Felicia. "Since you're so interested in history, that is a bit of culinary history."

Felicia had a way of weaving her displeasure into the conversation in the most indirect manner. Marie chose to turn the table.

"Culinary history is certainly important," said Marie. "Although it isn't explored as much. You will have to give me the recipe."

"You have never cooked anything in your life. That is what I mean by independence. Life skills."

"I just offered to cook tonight. I know how to order in a restaurant; that's a life skill."

"You're impossible. I don't know what kind of job you'll get after graduation."

Marie knew her mother still harbored disappointment about not having gone to art school, so she chose to drop the subject. There was a certain satisfaction for Marie in goading her mother, but she had to tread lightly. Everyone had limits.

"You know I think you should do what you want," said Felicia as she loaded the groceries into the car. "But it has to be within reason. You do not want to end up without prospects. You need to live in the real world."

"I know, Mom, but I just want to explore my options."

Her daughter's determination exasperated her. Felicia's other children were set on careers that would generate funds and new opportunities. Why couldn't Marie aspire to the same?

"I want all of you to get an education, but I don't want you to flounder," said Felicia.

"I won't flounder. I'm not the floundering type," Marie said. "Let's get these groceries home."

Marie was packing her case to return to New York City when Angela came into her room.

"I have something for you," said Angela. "This is a St. Christopher medal for protection on your travels." She put it around Marie's neck.

"But I'm only going back to school. And I'm not religious."

"It is for protection on your life's journey," said Angela. "Like the lions on my mantle, it will protect you from mishaps when you travel, whether inside your mind or on the earth."

"Thank you," said Marie. "I have never seen you wear this medal," said Marie.

"The nuns in Palermo gave it to me, and I wore it on my journey to this country and when I returned to Sicily in 1929. Now it is yours. I won't be traveling anymore, but you will."

"Are you ready?" asked Felicia. "Hurry and pack your bag. You'll miss your train."

Marie kissed her aunt and said goodbye. She had always wanted to travel, but college came first.

Angela felt lighter after she had relinquished her St. Christopher medal. She had all the protection she needed from her unseen friends and her lions. Her preservation did not come from an object. She felt that passing it down to Marie added extra security to a young life just beginning, as hers was waning. Angela was in the dormitory packing for her voyage to America when the nuns presented her with the medal.

"Angela," said one of the nuns, "we have something for you."

A group of the sisters stood around her. The nun who spoke stepped forward and presented her with the St. Christopher medal.

"This is for protection on your travels. This way you take us with you—your family."

Now, almost sixty years later, Angela had a new family and had passed on the love and connection she was gifted at the beginning of her journey.

After Marie and Felicia left for the train station, Angela decided to clean her sewing area. She swept the floor and dusted and oiled the sewing machine cabinet. She sprayed the mirror with glass cleaner, removing the dust that prevented her from seeing clearly. Her sister-in-law, Speranza, had spent many hours in front of the mirror as Angela pinned her garments—some celebratory, others pedestrian. The garment that combined both celebration and sadness was Speranza's wedding gown. Angela had wanted to pretend she was happy about her marriage to Salvatore, but she could not. Now Angela wished she had been happy for her sister-in-law to give her a boost, regardless of how she felt. The image captured in the mirror was one of sadness for Angela.

Other memories embedded in the mirror were humorous. She had fitted Sadie with a new blouse and skirt upon Sadie's request because she was tired of some of the women gossiping about her well-worn outfit. She wanted Angela to make the same black skirt and white blouse to shut up the gossipers. Try as she might, Angela could not convince Sadie to consider different clothes. Angela did, however, get Sadie to buy a new pair of elastic stockings because the pair she wore drooped at the knees and ankles.

Then there was the multitude of stylish women who came to Angela to seek her advice on what would look the best for a dinner, luncheon, or evening gala. Her ability to transform an ordinary design into a reflection of what the client aspired to be was what brought her clients. These images of metamorphosis were also submerged in the mirror's landscape. These figures carried more lightness, so they came forward more easily and inspired creativity instead of regret or sadness. The memories with family held more weight. Angela felt she had achieved a balance in her clients and designs. She wondered how many more years she had left to sew. Maybe she would not smash the mirror so those in its inner landscape would live as they were, without aging or illness.

The phone rang, snapping Angela out of her daydream.

"Oh, hello, Joe," said Angela. "How are you doing? How was London?"

"Dick and I had a wonderful time. I wanted to visit you this weekend."

"We would love to have you. Why don't you stay overnight?"

"All right. Dick will be out of town on business."

"Ok, I'll see you this weekend. Felicia will pick you up Saturday morning."

Having Joe around was like having his mother Speranza back. Angela was sure Speranza would have been proud of Joe and how he rose above his childhood. Angela always treated Joe and Marie similarly: they could do no wrong. She was delighted that Marie had inherited Joe's interest in travel and the opportunities in Manhattan.

When Angela reflected on her marriage, there was a weight of disappointment that bound her to the past. She had transcended much in her life, but one truth about her life in America was a wound that would open occasionally to remind her of its presence. After World War II and her nephew Nunzio's death, she had buried her resentment for his loss. She felt he had died in Hiroshima along with his men, even though he had survived the trauma. When he came home, he was a shell and was unable to climb out of a deep dark space. The fact that she had gotten Captain Bonifice to bring his son Robert home through bribery gave her more than just satisfaction: it taught her those with power were not untouchable.

"Hi, Angela," said Felicia. She had just returned from work and carried a pile of large envelopes.

"You brought work home again," said Angela. "They should pay you for that."

"We're just so busy I couldn't get to all the paperwork. Title companies are busy."

"Listen, Joe is coming this weekend. His birthday is soon, so I thought we'd have a cake."

"All right. I'll make veal," said Felicia. "He'll like that."

It was a good day for Felicia when her brother-in-law visited. It was a time to relax, enjoy his dry sense of humor, and experience life through his perceptions. He would talk about his travels and New York life. Andrea came in and threw off her jacket and books.

"Take those upstairs," said Felicia. "You shouldn't throw your things around like that."

"Maybe we should let Marie know that Joe will be here this weekend and they could come together on the train," said Angela.

"Marie was just here," said Felicia. "She may have plans with her friends."

"I will invite Paolina," said Angela. "Joe enjoys Paolina."

Angela had already invited Salvatore's sister, Paolina. She was Joe's aunt, and Angela felt that it was important for extended family to get together.

"All right," said Felicia. "I will shop tomorrow."

Angela's feelings of resentment toward Paolina had softened over the years. There was a time Paolina's presence would cause Angela's blood pressure to rise, and then she would hyperventilate because Paolina had encouraged the relationship between her brother, Salvatore, and Speranza. But she was now able to view her as an amusing dinner companion.

On Saturday morning, Joe carried two leather bags as he and Felicia walked through the front door.

"Aunt Angela, I'm here," Joe said.

"Oh, I'm so glad to see you, Joe," said Angela. "Put your bags down."

She embraced him and stood back as if she was stepping back to observe a sculpture she had created.

"How do you like my new suit?" He unbuttoned his jacket and displayed the interior. "All Italian silk, even better than my last Armani. It is this season."

"It is beautiful," said Angela. She examined the seams and touched the silk as she lifted the jacket. "It has good weight, and the silk is the finest. Perfectly tailored." Tailoring this refined made Angela feel that the world still possessed a semblance of order and tradition. "I am so glad you are looking so well. Why have you brought two bags for an overnight visit?"

"I have to have a change of clothes, shoes, and my personal items. Felicia, thank you for picking me up."

"Sure," said Felicia. "I have to go back to work. I'll see everyone later."

"Your Aunt Paolina is coming for dinner tonight," said Angela.

"Really? I think she's a riot," said Joe, lighting a Gauloises cigarette.

"Put your bags in my sitting room and come in the dining room for some coffee," said Angela.

A plush sofa sat facing the marble fireplace, and piles of fabric were neatly piled on a table in the center of the sitting room. It was a large room off Angela's bedroom that contained sewing remnants, patterns, and a desk. Joe remembered sitting on the couch with Angela as a child and listening to her stories. As he grew, she had talked about his mother and how much she missed her. He found these conversations tedious, needing to look forward in his life and not drown in someone else's pain. He had his own pain to contend with because of his mother's death. When he left Nelsonville to make a life in New York City, he'd never looked back.

But like most of his family members, he owed a debt of gratitude to Angela. She had stepped up when his mother died and had taught him to cook and to speak Italian. Joe took off his Armani suit jacket, hung it in the closet, and ran his hand down the front as if it were an exotic pet.

"Coffee is ready," said Angela. She opened the French doors to the sitting room that opened into the dining room. Bright sun streamed in through the windows, creating a spotlight on the photographs sitting on the buffet. Joe walked over to the buffet.

"You still have these pictures," Joe said.

He picked up a black and white photograph of his mother, maternal grandmother, and Angela.

"That was taken in 1914," said Angela, "not long after I arrived in this country. You mother is about ten in that picture."

Angela was standing behind Speranza with her hands on her young sister-in-law's shoulders. Angela looked to the right slightly while Franco's mother peered into the camera. It was the image of an immigrant family frozen in time at the precipice of a new life in America.

"My mother looks happy," said Joe. "I was five when she died. That was a long time ago."

"Well, she was a jolly person," said Angela. "She was always smiling. You have her sense of humor."

After his mother died, his life had been derailed onto a new timeline. The house felt empty and when his father, Salvatore, went to Sicily and married his seventeen-year-old niece, Joe had begun his plan his escape from Nelsonville.

"I remember once when my mother forgot to make dinner," said Joe. She played with my brother, my sister and me all day, and the time just flew by. My father came home and expected dinner to be ready. We laughed and laughed. She loved fun."

"She liked to play practical jokes on everyone," said Angela. "Once she hid under my bed and I looked for her for a half hour. I called your grandmother to see if she had gone out, when suddenly she came out and nearly scared me to death."

"That sounds like her," Joe said.

Angela poured the coffee and sliced the cake.

"Are you happy?" Angela asked.

"Yes, I have a good life. Dick and I travel and buy what we want. It's the life I had always imagined. Dick makes good money as a producer, and we have a rent control apartment on the East Side."

"I am glad. You deserve it after what you went through as a child. No one knows more than me."

"You were there for me and helped me when I moved to New York. I'll never forget."

Moments like these validated her purpose in life: to assist her family in achieving their dreams. She experienced a deep satisfaction when one of the people she had cared for became happy and successful.

"It was my pleasure," said Angela. She poured the coffee and handed Joe a piece of cake.

"Have you seen Marie in the city?" asked Angela.

"No, I haven't seen her. I figure she is involved with school and prefers hanging out with friends. She's the independent type and very much like her mother."

"Yes, she is," said Angela. She smiled to herself, knowing that her influence stretched into Marie's consciousness. She may appear like her mother on the surface, thought Angela, but outer appearances were superfluous. It was underneath the shell that Angela had molded.

"Your mother, you, and Marie are the same," said Angela.

"The same? What do you mean?"

"All of you are simpatico," said Angela. She sipped her coffee and waited for Joe's response.

Joe paused and searched his memory for anything that would connect the three generations. He had been close to his mother and preferred her company to his father, but that was a brief amount of time to draw any connections. Marie had been his favorite niece because he found her to be engaging.

"I never had children," said Angela, "but I will live on in you and Marie. That is what I will leave here on earth."

"You are not going anywhere yet," said Joe, snuffing out his cigarette. "You'll die at your sewing machine. Maybe we can bury it with you."

"See, you have your mother's wicked sense of humor. Many people do not understand it."

"Well, if you can't take a joke…"

"How is Dick?" asked Angela. "How is his business doing?"

"Dick is producing two more movies. That should set us up for life."

"I am glad you are not alone," said Angela. "You have found a partner."

"I think I will rest before dinner," said Joe. "I want to be fresh as a daisy for our guest."

"Go in and lie down on the couch in the sitting room," said Angela. "I am going to prepare the cheesecake."

"Sounds yummy," said Joe. He kissed Angela on both cheeks and disappeared into the sitting room.

Joe awoke and looked at his watch. It was four o'clock and time to get up and prepare for the evening. He heard Angela working in the kitchen, and the aroma of sautéed onions and garlic permeated the air. He remembered a time he had awakened from a nap as a child and walked into the kitchen to find his mother sautéing garlic. She had looked down and smiled at him, and a feeling home and safety had enveloped his body. He hugged her, and she smoothed his hair back, bent down and kissed the top of his head. That was the most tender memory he had of his mother. There was no one else around, just he and Speranza with a shared moment that belonged to him. Joe dressed and went upstairs to see Felicia.

"Felicia, are you busy?" he called. He stood at the top of the stairs and gazed in the hall mirror and ran his fingers through his hair. He was dressed in his country black slacks, Gucci loafers, and a tailored red shirt.

"In the living room," Felicia responded.

"I wanted to come up and see how you're doing."

"Nice shirt," Felicia kissed him on the cheek.

"I bought it in Rome last year. We flew Alitalia. Boy, that was an experience. All airlines are bad, but when you fly Alitalia, they throw things at you."

They laughed and sat on the couch.

"I'm glad the children are doing well. I tell people I love my sister-in-law and that she has done such a fantastic job with the family."

"Thank you, Joe," said Felicia. She wondered if he was saying that because he did not want to have to deal with Angela as she aged, cr if he meant it.

"We have been friends for a long time, and I wanted to say…"

"Hey, Uncle Joe," said Andrea, "when did you get here?"

"A while ago. Look how grown up you are. You look like you're ready to take on the world." Andrea wore a red, cotton one-piece slack set with platform shoes. The red complemented her black hair, olive skin and fiery personality.

Andrea smiled and brimmed with energy.

"I heard Aunt Paolina is coming tonight," said Andrea.

"Yes, and we'll have some fun with her," said Joe.

"Make sure you hang up your clothes," said Felicia.

"Can I go out after dinner?" asked Andrea.

"Go and hang up your clothes. We are visiting with your uncle," Felicia said.

Andrea grumbled and left to change.

"Wear something fun and sassy," said Joe.

Joe was adept at cutting tension in any situation, with a talent for making peace and redirecting an uncomfortable moment. Joe had learned to do this at an early age when his father had married his own niece, Immacolatta. Joe had longed for a mother after his mother passed and saw potential in his father's new bride. When his stepmother had children, he endeared himself to her by helping her care for the children.

She found him to be an invaluable asset in the household, but she ultimately took advantage of his need to be loved.

One day, after Angela had observed the situation, she had taken Joe by the hand and brought him to live in the house on Morning Glory Avenue. Joe was grateful and learned he had to do extraordinarily little to illicit praise from Angela.

"Felicia, I wanted to say I appreciate you picking me up from the station every time I visit. You have been a godsend to this family. I wish my brother was alive to see how well you've raised the children."

"Thank you, Joe. I do my best, and Angela is a great help."

"We have both struggled to become who we are; we know what it takes."

"I focus on what I have, not what I have lost," said Felicia.

"It's best to focus on the future," said Joe. "Not what didn't work in the past. Sometimes it is good to walk away from your previous life."

"Let's go downstairs and see if we can raid the liquor cabinet," said Joe. "I need a drink. Will you join me?"

"Have I ever said no?"

Angela served veal cutlets and pasta Bolognese. Paolina and Joe sat across from one another.

"Paolina, let me fill your plate," said Joe. He dug the serving fork into the pasta and piled a huge amount on Paolina's plate. His father's sister had always been a big eater.

"That enough," said Paolina. "You are going to make me fat." Like many older Italian ladies, she had expanded over the years.

"Oh, come on, you still have your girlish figure," said Joe.

"You are funny," said Paolina. "You know I should lose weight."

"You still look good," said Joe. "Just stand up and be who you are."

Most people who spent time with Joe fell in love with him and his charm. Waiters, shop girls, or anyone in his orbit found him to be endearing and marvelous company. He knew that Angela could never completely forgive his father for marrying his own niece after his mother's death, but he believed that families should stay together regardless of mistakes. Immacolatta and Salvatore had moved out of Nelsonville to Queens, New York ten years ago, and the distance helped ease tensions.

"You are just charming me," said Paolina.

"He is like his mother," said Angela. "Everyone loved Speranza. She had an interest in people, and so does our Joe."

Paolina cleared her throat, making her voice ready for a retort in case Angela chastised her about supporting Salvatore when he went to Sicily to marry Immacolatta.

"So, have you remarried, Aunt Paolina?" asked Joe. "I'm sure a woman like you would have no problem."

"Look at Felicia," said Paolina. "She is attractive, and she is still single even through her husband died twelve years ago."

"I don't need to be married," said Felicia. For Felicia it was tiring when people asked why she had not remarried. This was 1970, and it was no longer necessary for a woman, certainly not a successful one, to be married.

"How about it, Felicia?" asked Joe. "No romance?"

"I'm much too busy. Besides, who wants to stay home and wash someone's clothes? And I will not have someone tell my children what to do. That's my job."

"I agree," said Joe. "I have our clothes sent out. I tell Dick: 'I am not a maid. If you want a maid, hire one.' You and me, Felicia, we think alike."

"I have to go out after dinner," said Andrea.

"Where are you going?" asked Felicia.

"Out with friends," said Andrea.

"You'd better not be late," said Felicia.

Andrea did not respond. She knew that silence would send her mother over the edge.

"Did you hear me?"

"How could I not hear you? You're sitting across the table. I'd have to be deaf."

"I'm sure she'll be home early," said Joe. "I thought we would sit on the porch later and tell stories. You wouldn't want to miss that."

"God no, I live for stories about people I've never met. See you later." Andrea chewed on an olive as she went out the side door.

"She's a firecracker," said Joe. "Both girls are so independent."

"She is like Speranza," said Angela. "I could never talk sense into her, either. She got married too young."

"Well," said Paolina. "She was in love with my brother, so why not get married?"

"Why not get married?" said Angela, her face turning red. "I can give you a few good reasons."

"Water under the bridge," said Joe. "It happened many years ago. Let's not bring up my mother."

"That's right, Joe," said Paolina. "One should not speak ill of the dead."

"Who is speaking ill of Speranza?" asked Angela. "I was just saying she was too young to get married. She was a wonderful person, and her death was a tragedy."

"Anyone want more veal?" asked Felicia.

"I'll take some," said Joe. "Come on, ladies, let us talk less about family and more about what's in store in the 1970s. It's a new decade."

Angela could not help but bring up Speranza. Having Paolina around brought up such anger in Angela that she thought she would have a stroke. She decided that for the rest of the dinner she would not speak about Speranza.

"You are right, Joe," said Angela. "It is a new world, and the past is gone, not to be revisited."

Chapter 8

BENEVOLENCE OF NEW IDEAS

1971

Marie had decided to stay in Manhattan once her freshman year ended at City College. Felicia refused to give her extra money for the summer, so Marie secured employment at Brentano's Books on Fifth Avenue across from the Lincoln Center. The manager took a liking to Marie and educated her about the workings of a bookstore. Still, living in New York City required more income than a bookstore salary.

On a weekend visit to Nelsonville, Angela overheard Felicia telling Marie that she would not contribute to her maintenance for her summer in Manhattan because she could easily come home and live for free until her classes started again in the fall. On Sunday, Angela slipped an envelope into Marie's pocket.

"What is this?" asked Marie. She reached into her pocket.

"Don't take it out. I know you need money," said Angela. "It is a little something for you to start your summer. Living in New York City is not cheap."

"Thank you, Aunt Angela. "This really helps."

"I helped your Uncle Joe when he left home, and I have never regretted the money I invested. Some people invest in houses, I invest in people."

"I'm not exactly a sure thing," said Marie.

"I only ask that you go for what you want and not be influenced by others."

"I can do that," said Marie.

Marie put her arms around her aunt, and Angela whispered something in her ear. Marie heard her mother's purposeful step in the hallway. She turned to find Felicia standing behind her, arms folded.

"What are you going to do today?" asked Felicia.

"I'm not sure. I thought I would go to the dude ranch and ride a bit. I can't afford to ride in Central Park."

"I should say not," said Felicia. "I must run some errands; care to join me?'

To Marie, the prospect of spending alone time with her mother was about as attractive as sitting in a lion's den. She took a deep breath and chose to see if she could tame the lion.

"I can always ride in the afternoon."

"Okay, I will see you two later," said Angela. "Bring back some ricotta, and I will make a ricotta cheesecake."

Marie looked back at Angela in time to see her aunt blow her a kiss. Everyone should have a woman like Angela in their lives, thought Marie. When she was a child, she thought everyone had a person like Angela in their household— someone who told stories, anticipated needs and expressed concern—but as she connected with students at college, she found a different reality: uncommunicative fathers, neglectful mothers, and fractured families. Some students did not have one dependable person in their lives. It was then that Marie realized her upbringing was unique. As a child, she had received ideas from her great aunt, just by observing, that were outside traditional teaching socially and spiritually.

Angela and Sadie sat on the porch for the afternoon and talked about the state of the world and all the changes that they had seen over the years—the good and the not so good. Some of the changes they did not understand but accepted anyway. It was in vogue for the youth to challenge authority in the 1960s and early 1970s, but Sicilians had challenged the ruling class and church doctrine for centuries. The difference was that Sicilians consistently lost, but the young Americans had the possibility of winning. Angela was glad she had lived to see the transformation of American society so that her nieces and nephews could become more of themselves.

"Women are going into law and medicine now," said Sadie. "When we were young, there were no women doctors or lawyers. Women do not have to marry to have stability."

"I guess not," said Angela. "My choices were limited, but my nieces will have more choices. Some of my clients say that women are applying and pushing to open doors at Yale—Harvard, too. I hope I live to see it."

"You are as healthy as a horse," said Sadie. "I'll be gone before you."

Angela had not thought about her own death, but it seemed that she was outliving many of her family and friends. Death had been her constant companion her entire life, but it never took her. Maybe she had outsmarted death after the earthquake. Most people perished during that disaster, but even after the earth settled, Messina's citizens either died from wounds sustained from falling buildings or they simply vanished. Children who were seen after the earth erupted disappeared and were never seen again. Angela had also heard that children were rounded up and sold into slavery.

After Franco's death, Angela was becoming more transparent in her practice of unconventional spirituality and search for connection with the unseen world. She angered priests and conservative friends, but persisted, even calling church practices into question.

"Mrs. Bellini," said the priest on the day of her husband's funeral, "can you contribute more to your husband's service today? It would go to supporting the church and the priests." He took a drag on his cigarette.

"Do you help the poor?" asked Angela.

"We pray for the poor, if that is what you mean."

"I mean, how much of the money you collect goes to the poor? That is God's work."

"God helps those who help themselves."

"If that is your belief, I am sure you will take that advice."

The priest never received the extra money, and Angela settled on praying at home at her altar of the Blessed Mother. She no longer had any use for the Catholic Church, but she still attended mass. There was something in the ritual that still drew her. The silence and meditative quality of praying with others seemed to deepen her connection with the unseen. She could hear them better because of the collective silence.

"Are you taking your water pill? Your ankles are so swollen," said Angela.

"Sometimes I take them," Sadie said as she rolled down her stocking. "I am having more trouble walking because my legs swell up. The doctor keeps telling me to stop drinking, but I love my wine. I want to enjoy my life."

"You should take care of yourself, no matter what."

"You have been a good friend, Angela. You have been good to me when others in our community thought less of me."

"Everyone's life is important, no matter what others say— even you. Besides, you can take a joke. That's why people marched for Civil Rights, because everyone's life matters."

Many in the Italian-American community held a quiet disdain for Sadie. Her disheveled appearance and blunt speech offended them. Angela understood her friend as an individual with a perspective to share, while most in the community considered her a joke. The wives did not like that she could sit and drink wine with their husbands and debate politics, while they remained silent.

"I have led the life I wanted," said Sadie.

Felicia and Marie came up the side stairs with groceries.

"I just mean, it is a time of exploring for me," said Marie, placing the groceries on the table.

"Explore on your own time," said Felicia. "How do you expect to make a living with a history degree?"

"So, where did you two love birds go?" asked Sadie.

"Shopping," said Marie. She opened the back door and slammed it behind her.

"She's being difficult, as usual," said Felicia. She began putting groceries away.

The phone rang.

"Oh, that must be my boyfriend," Sadie teased.

"I will get it," said Angela.

"Hello, Captain Bonifice," Angela said. "How are you?"

"Yes, you can come by... Why don't you and your wife come for dinner? I would like to repay your kindness. We missed her the last time. Would next Friday evening suit you? I will invite the Gallucis. I am sure you remember them from our dinners years ago."

"Wonderful, we will see you at seven."

"Who was that?" asked Sadie.

"We are having dinner next Friday with the Bonifices and Gallucis. He's thinking of running for political office and would like to talk to us about it."

"A fly on the wall. I want to be a fly on the wall."

"Sadie, you will have to sit this dinner out. I want to thank him again for helping Robert, but I'm curious about why he wants to talk to us," said Angela.

"You know a lot of people," said Sadie. "Besides, he helped you with Robert, so he wants you to help him. You know how it works; he wants you to spread the word. *Arrivederci*."

Given Angela's affluent clientele, she had the ear of well-connected women who had influence over their husbands. It would make sense that he would ask for Angela's support. She walked over to the hall window and watched as Sadie descended the stairs, taking one step at a time, shoulders hunched, tightly holding the railing. Angela thought about time and how it had sneaked past her like a thief in darkness. Her unseen friends told her there was no linear time where they resided. One day they would both die, she and Sadie, but she believed that if one person remembers and appreciates you for your time on earth, then no one dies.

That night, Sadie went to bed and died peacefully in her sleep.

"I found her this morning," said Sadie's daughter. "I hope you don't mind me calling you."

"Not at all. I am so sorry," said Angela. "She was a good friend and made everyone's life happier."

"The funeral home should be here soon."

"If you need to go and make arrangements with the church, I will stay with your mother."

"Thank you, Angela. My mother really loved you."

Angela opened the door to where Sadie lay. The sheet was drawn over her head, and her tattered clothes were neatly folded on a chair. An unopened bottle of wine, a corkscrew, and wine glass sat on her night table. Death must have come early in the evening, because ordinarily Sadie would have enjoyed her wine. Angela gently lifted the sheet off Sadie's face, opened the bottle of wine and poured some in the glass. Sadie's face was serene. The stress of life had drained away, and now she was ready to enter the unseen realm.

"*Alla tua!*" Angela lifted the glass, drank it down, and kissed her friend's forehead. "Safe travels, and be guided by the angels."

Angela looked around to take a souvenir to remind her of their friendship. She settled on the bottle of wine, walked toward the door, and turned to look at Sadie for the last time. Tears rolled down her cheeks as she realized she would no longer enjoy her visits, phone conversations or laughter. Life just got a little quieter and lonelier.

On Friday, Angela and Felicia finished setting the table for dinner.

"It is sad to think that Sadie won't sit at the table any-more," said Felicia.

"She will be here tonight. I am serving the wine that was on her bedside table."

The doorbell rang, and Angela opened the door for Gianni and Ramina Galluci. Both large people, they announced their presence with their inflated chests. Ramina wore a fur coat and shiny dangly earrings. Her face was generously powdered, and she wore pink lipstick. Hair perfectly coiffed, her voice was so high it was like nails dragged across a blackboard.

"Ramina, Gianni come in." Angela kissed the couple on both cheeks.

"We are looking forward to visiting with Captain Bonifice," said Ramina as she took off her coat. "Sadie's funeral was genuinely nice. You must miss her."

"Every day," said Angela. "But God took her, so she is at rest."

During Sadie's lifetime, the Gallucis had never invited her to join them for dinner. But that was not what tonight was about. Angela had invited the Gallucis because they shared many of Captain Bonifice's political views. It would put him at ease so he could present his intensions.

Felicia received the Bonifices as they arrived and showed them into the dining room as Angela directed them to their places at the dining room table. She had presided over countless dinners during her years at Morning Glory Avenue. Some were mundane, others revealed hidden patterns of darkness, and some had an atmosphere saturated with joy. Angela could usually sense how an evening would go, but tonight was a clouded mystery. She could not see beyond the moment.

"You both know Ramina and Gianni," said Angela.

"It is good to see you both," said Arthur. He took off his suit jacket and vigorously shook their hands.

"How are you doing, Captain?" asked Gianni. "Haven't seen you in a while."

"Soon to be major," said Lucy, holding her husband's arm.

"I have to admit I have an ulterior motive for coming tonight," said the captain. "Before we talk about that, I am looking forward to Angela's cooking."

"Arthur, I have heard you are running for New York State Assembly Representative," Felicia said. "I am surprised; the military has been your career."

"My husband needs the support of the community, and since your husband worked with Arthur, we thought you might have an interest." Lucy Bonifice's grandparents had been textile workers from Piedmont in Italy and were considered laborers. Northern laborers who immigrated to America held a lower status than southerners who immigrated as craftspeople, like Angela and Franco. Lucy had worked hard to overcome the stigma, and she taught their American-born children to climb the social ladder.

"I didn't know you could run for office if you were in the military," said Felicia.

"I am in the Reserves," said Arthur. "If you are active duty, you are prohibited."

"You are lucky," said Ramina. "You will have a higher rank, and then you might run for Senate."

Angela remained silent and recalled what Nunzio had once told her: "The military will be running politics in the future."

"Do you think it is wise to mix politics with the military?" asked Felicia. "One is to defend, and the other to make laws that serve the people."

Angela had learned what the military was about through Nunzio. She knew there were many men who lost their souls and lives to defending freedom but had not attained freedom for themselves; it had been stolen by their unquestioning commitment to government.

"What do you think of the protests against the Vietnam War?" asked Gianni.

"I think they need to be stopped," said the captain. "They disrupt society."

"Maybe the people are expressing their views against a government that wants war for its own purposes," Angela said.

"That is a liberal point of view," said Arthur. "My platform will focus on protecting America from the Communists. That is why we are fighting in Asia."

The same feelings she had during World War II swelled up inside her like a tsunami. She remembered Sarah Einbinder's reminder that Henry Ford was getting rich through selling vehicles to the Nazis. She was sure someone was getting rich through the Vietnam War.

"And since this is America, I can express any view I like. Isn't that true?" Angela could hear Sadie laughing and applauding her. Was he really going to ask for her support?

"Absolutely, Angela, we all have different opinions, but I'm sure we can all agree that we don't want to live under Communist rule. The boys who are brave enough to fight will prevent that from happening."

"Courage comes in many forms," said Angela. "The ones who protest have courage to go against the system. Even those who refuse to fight." She wanted to make sure he remembered that he pulled strings to bring Robert home.

"Tell us about your campaign," said Ramina.

As Angela and Felicia brought out the main course, Arthur continued to explain how he would support less government and cut unnecessary welfare programs.

"Too much money is wasted," said Gianni with a mouth full of pasta.

"I have my convictions, and I do not stray from them," Arthur stated.

"Here, here," said Gianni. "We need more men in government like you."

"Thank you for your support."

To Angela, the word "conviction" suggested a court case and that the verdict was issued with a trial. There was no room for discussion or exchange of ideas. Angela saw that a tactful approach was needed for the evening.

"Felicia, what do you think," said Arthur. "Nunzio would have agreed with me."

"I don't know who he would have agreed with. The world has changed."

"He defended his country well," said Arthur.

"Well, Arthur," said Angela, "we have to look at all the policies presented by all the candidates. It is our duty as Americans to do that. I am sure you agree. After all, that is why your parents immigrated to this country." Angela used his first name because it put her on a level playing field, and she knew it endeared her to him.

"Yes, of course."

"Then we are agreed," Angela raised her glass to him.

"You have my and my wife's vote, Captain Bonifice," said Gianni.

Ramina looked at her husband and said nothing.

"What do you think of draft dodgers?" Ramina asked.

"I am opposed to them. I think they should be punished. My generation fought willingly, and we were triumphant," said Arthur.

"Congratulations on your rise to the rank of major," said Angela.

"They are considering me. It's not definite."

Angela brought out the dessert and more wine. She kept filling the captain's glass throughout the dinner, as she encouraged him to talk about his policies, women's equality and civil rights.

"So, ladies, I would like to ask for your support. Angela, I know that you are acquainted with many women whose husbands support the Republican ticket. Would you be averse to letting them know that I am running for state representative and vouch for my character? I can have my assistant deliver some flyers."

"I do not mix politics with doing business. I cannot suggest a candidate to my clients." Angela knew Captain Bonifice had gotten deferments for the sons of her wealthy clients and they would already be happy to give him their vote.

"Would you be able to leave my flyers on a table for your clients? You do not have to endorse me. As an Italian-American community, we help each other even if we disagree." He lifted his eyebrows.

Angela paused.

"Yes, but I am sure your campaign will be successful without my help," said Angela. "My clients come here to relax and focus on clothing. I do not think it would sit well with them if I appeared to attempt to sway their vote." The owing of favors was traditional in Sicilian culture and American politics. Angela did not call on a favor when she persuaded Arthur Bonifice to help Robert; she called on his complicit involvement in taking money for political favors. Her clients had to pay to get their sons and nephews exempt from serving in Vietnam. If they knew that Angela held that over the captain's head to bring Robert home free of charge, they would not respond well.

"What is your position on women's rights?" asked Angela.

"I don't think women need a position," said Arthur. "They raise children and can have a little job when the children have grown."

Women's rights were becoming a concern in America, and her clients would want to know his position. If her clients asked, she could clearly convey his position.

"I will remind my clients that you are running for office. That should be sufficient to remind them to vote for who they want."

"You have always been an astute woman," said the captain. "Felicia, how about you? Does your office vote Republican? Maybe I could come in and speak to the employees. Can you mention it to your boss?"

"I don't really know how people vote. We are extremely busy this time of year." Felicia had no intention of getting involved in someone's political run.

"I have heard the FBI came looking for Robert," said the captain's wife. "He was trying to avoid the draft."

"Yes, they did," said Angela. "My niece, Marie, talked to them. It was a mistake. Wasn't it, Captain?"

Captain Bonifice hesitated and looked into the eyes of the other guests and hostesses. There was only one answer that was sustainable.

"Yes, it was a mistake."

"It's nice that he is home," Ramina said. "He was given medical leave anyway. Right, Angela? Where are the children tonight?"

"They are not children anymore," said Felicia. "I have two in college, Robert is designing tiles, and Andrea is in her high school senior year. She has decided to study retail merchandising."

"You have done an exemplary job," said the captain.

Lucy Bonifice announced that it was time to go, and the Gallucis and Bonifices said their goodbyes. Angela and Felicia walked their guests to the door.

"Do you think he will ever come back?" asked Felicia.

"I did not think so the last time he was here, but he returned. One day he will ask a favor from the wrong person."

Marie started her day at Brentano's in a one-piece orange pantsuit with short sleeves. It was one of the first garments she had purchased off racks in Manhattan. She enjoyed the hunt when she shopped for clothes; mining the racks for that perfect dress, selecting the color that would complement her skin, and trying on ready-made garments. Females worldwide were participating in the same ritual and they were connected through this ritual. Marie had a job, a shared apartment on West End Avenue and possibly a bright future in academics. She also had distance from her family. Her dream of living in New York City came true, so now she would make her own way to her future.

Marie was on a ladder shelving books when a young man in a T-shirt and jeans sauntered into the store. He came down the aisle where she was working and began checking out the titles. He pulled a book off the shelf and perused its pages, occasionally looking up at Marie as she stocked the top shelf.

"Where are the law books?" asked the young man.

"We don't have many. You should go to a law school bookstore."

"I'm a law student at Columbia. I was walking in the area, so I thought I'd check out your stock."

"They're hidden in a corner. I'll take you."

Marie climbed down the ladder.

"I'm Marie." Once she briefly touched his hand, he felt familiar even though she had never met him. There was an intimacy that she could not place.

"Josh."

"The law books are over here. What kind of law will you practice?"

"I'm thinking about environmental protection."

"I'm sure we'll be needing environmental lawyers in the future."

They walked down the aisle and turned left.

"See, slim pickings," Marie said. She liked how his black hair flopped over his eyes and his smile slanted to one side, giving him a disheveled look.

"Let me know if you need any more help." Marie turned to walk away.

"Thanks. What do you do when you're not here?"

Marie turned back, focused on Josh, and paused for a moment. She was not sure how much she should reveal to a stranger.

"I'm a student at City College, a sophomore."

"I'm third year law. I graduate in May. Do you live on the West Side?"

He seemed younger than a third-year law student.

"Yes, on West End Avenue."

"Would you like to have a drink at the West End Bar sometime? I live near Columbia, so we're practically neighbors."

The West End Bar was a hangout for the intelligentsia of the West Side. She figured a public place for a first meeting would be fine.

"That would be nice."

This would be Marie's first official date. High school boys had never interested her; she preferred someone with more experience and a bit more polish. Her aunt suggested she find someone who was "dainty." Marie translated that to mean cultural and educated. Josh was scruffy by design, but he obviously had goals in life.

"Great. We can get together tonight if you are available."

"I can meet you at seven," said Marie. "I do not eat meat, but I hear they have massive burgers."

Marie felt she spent much of her energy appeasing her mother and living up to her aunt's expectations. Angela had put a lot of energy into her over the years and she did not want to disappoint her, so she committed herself to her studies and work. Now she would enter the world of dating.

Since she had moved to New York, the only men that seemed interested in her were usually twenty years her senior. She did not understand why boys her own age never asked her out. With Josh, she had an opportunity to engage with someone her own age.

The West End Bar was packed with students, professors, and residents of the Upper West Side. A cloud of smoke rose over the bar as customers took drags from cigarettes between sips from scotch glasses. As Marie looked for Josh above the muffled sounds of conversation, she noticed that one couple was deep into a heated discussion. The woman stormed off, leaving her dinner partner yelling for her to return.

"Lively, isn't it?"

Marie turned around and saw Josh smiling. He wore an oversized sweater and jeans and look comfortably stylish.

"Yeah, not sure if we can get a table."

"There's a table in the corner," said Josh.

"This is luck."

Marie ordered a salad, and Josh ordered a cheeseburger.

"What is your major?" asked Josh.

"History, and do not ask me what I'm going to do with it."

"Wasn't going to. Parental concerns?"

"My mom. She is not happy with my choice. Your parents must be happy you're in law school."

"It suits me. I have clerked for some important judges, and yes, they are happy with my choices. What about your father?"

Marie felt a flush creep across her cheeks. She did not have the prospects that Josh had, and not having a father made her feel vulnerable. Josh's life was laid out in front of him, and from his confident demeanor, he was sure to be a success.

"My father died when I was six. I did not really know him. Your path is clear. I have a long way to go."

"I'm sorry; that must have been hard. I am amazed you did so well. I am sure you will find your way."

The truth was, it did not feel hard to Marie. She had had little connection with her father, and no one talked about him after his death; he was there one day and then he was gone. It seemed to Marie that no one wanted to keep his memory alive. She had heard friends talk about their deceased grandparents with longing. They told vivid stories about memories or trips to Disneyland. Her friends drew from these memories to keep their grandparents present in their lives. Once Nunzio was gone, it seemed it was best to keep him gone.

Josh and Marie talked about their hopes and goals for the future. Josh lived a few blocks away in an apartment owned by Columbia University. Marie lived on West 99th Street and West End Avenue with a roommate.

"Do you like your job? It must be difficult working and carrying a full course load. I don't think I could do it."

"You do what you have to do,'" said Marie.

"You're strong. I like that."

"I was raised by strong women."

Marie saw her mother and aunt as strong, but not herself. When she was younger, she had allowed people to take advantage of her. She often wondered why she felt compelled to say yes to people even when it went against what she wanted. This had been a pattern she had struggled with since she was first aware of it at age five. She realized it diverted attention away from her to comply.

After a few hours, Josh kissed Marie as they stood outside the restaurant.

"Busy this weekend?" asked Josh.

"I'm going to Nelsonville to visit my family, but I'll be back late Sunday morning."

They parted company after making plans to see each other on Sunday evening.

Marie stood in the center of Grand Central Station and looked up at the constellations painted on the ceiling. It felt appropriate to her that a building that housed travel had the guide to the heavens spread across its ceiling like a city map. Whenever Marie traveled, she tapped into a feeling of wander-lust, whether that involved journeying through the narrow streets of Greenwich Village or train travel. Wandering though train stations and New York streets connected her to the possibilities in her life, and this was magnified by the celestial mural above her. The expansive feeling was difficult to articulate, but it was there inside her. She felt that the mural reflected her inner landscape.

The fall semester had had started, and she wanted to visit her family before she was inundated with writing papers and working at the bookstore. She was leaning more toward a creative career, but she was not sure what that meant or how she would express it. She found her lack of focus unsettling but was more concerned about her mother's wrath.

"I will drop you at home, then I'll be back to make dinner," said Felicia as she pulled away from the Nelsonville train station.

"Great, I will spend time with Aunt Angela."

"If she offers you money, don't take it. She has done enough. How is your job going?"

"I'm learning a lot."

"What about school? Did you pick a major yet?"

"Almost. I think by the end of this semester I should know exactly what I want to do."

"So, you haven't chosen history as your major?"

"There is no need to declare one just yet."

"That is good news. Why not major in nursing? If you do well enough you could get a master's degree in nursing."

"I'll think about it."

It was best to tell her mother what she wanted to hear. As Felicia pulled into the driveway, Marie saw Angela standing on the porch.

"I have been waiting for you," said Angela. She put her arms around Marie, but it felt different. It was not a grasp that drew Marie into her like when she was a child. There seemed to be more detachment; a hug that had matured into a delicate embrace.

"I have missed you so much," said Angela. "We did not see you much over the summer."

"I am busy at the bookstore."

"I hope you have been enjoying yourself. Uncle Joe said you will be meeting with him once he returns from London."

"Yes, we'll have brunch."

"Dress up nicely. No jeans. What else have you been doing in New York?"

Ever the fashionista, thought Marie. She imagined that if Angela were her age, she would be attending the Fashion Institute of Technology.

"I did have a date."

"Tell me about him."

Angela took Marie by the arm and escorted her to the kitchen.

"Who is this boy?" Angela poured the espresso into vintage demitasse cups. The hand-painted cups had been in the family for as long as she could remember: two Renaissance ladies playing with a small child in a pastoral scene.

"There is nothing much to tell. We just met. He is a law student at Columbia."

"A law student? You must tell your mother. She will be pleased."

"We have only had one date. No need to do that. She'll imagine that we'll get married."

"When will you see him again?"

"On Sunday evening."

"That will be our secret," said Angela. "I have a doctor's appointment across the street now. Make yourself a sandwich if you get hungry. I won't be long."

"Do you want me to come with you?"

"No, it's just for my arthritis. He gives me medicine for it."

The house felt smaller than Marie remembered. It had only been a couple of months since her last visit, but the walls seemed to be closer together and the furniture a bit cramped, but nothing externally had changed. The furniture was in the same place and the wall color had not changed. Marie did feel different since she had moved to New York. She was living in a much smaller space, but she had the entire city to explore. Nelsonville itself seemed congested, as did her ancestral home.

On the dining room buffet, she saw the picture of her father in his Marine uniform on his wedding day twenty-seven years earlier. Nothing moved from its spot in this home on Morning Glory Avenue. To Marie, it was starting to feel and look like a time warp. It was 1971, but the early 20th century was still solidly present—not quite museum-like, but on its way. She wondered if one could make past decades and centuries come alive through objects and photos. History appealed to her, but dwelling in the past did not. It was time to look toward the future.

"I'm back," said Angela as she took off her jacket. "The doctor gave me some cream for my hands. I want to keep sewing, and it helps."

"Have you ever thought of retiring?"

"No. This is what I do and who I am. You do not stop being who you are. Everyone needs work."

"I suppose," said Marie. "You know who you are."

"No, I am just myself."

Marie thought that maybe if she were herself, she would realize what she was supposed to be doing with her life.

"You are so lucky you found your talent when you were young and made a business out of it. How did you know that dressmaking was your talent? Did you ever want to do something else?"

"I sewed at the convent and used that skill when I came to this country. When I started sewing for the nuns at St. Mary's School, I saw that I was more skilled than the other women who sewed linens. That is when I realized that I could make money if I had the right customers. The other women treated me poorly because they felt I was showing them up, and the nuns would expect them to be at my skill level. It was a great lesson for me."

"What was the lesson?"

"Don't be with people who expect you to be less than you are."

"I think about my future," said Marie. "It should be more certain, but it's not."

"That's all right. It will come to you. You must take a chance. I did not have the benefit of thinking I could do anything else. Do not be in a hurry to choose, and do not tell your mother I said that. Maybe you could write my story."

"That is funny, because after working at the bookstore I thought I could become a writer."

"I think maybe you could. Listen to the voice inside. I have listened to my voices and they have not failed me, but it does not mean it will be easy."

The frustration Marie felt could not be solved by picking a major but needed to be remedied from the inside.

"I'll start dinner. Your mother will be home in an hour. I left new dress patterns on my bed. Some of them may interest you."

Marie went into the hallway and was about to separate the French doors to Angela's room when she glanced at the full-length mirror. She touched the mirror's gold frame and stepped up on the platform. Because of Angela's warnings, she was once again afraid to stare directly into the mirror's vast space— as if it would swallow her up. The way to quell the fear is a matter of control, thought Marie, and detachment would aid in exploring the mirror's landscape. Like Alice and the looking glass, Marie was born to delve into other times and spaces on planet earth.

"I thought you might like this material with one of the patterns," said Angela from behind her.

She stopped and gazed at Marie standing in front of the mirror. Angela did not scold or warn Marie about the mirror's dangers. Angela had protected Marie from unseen forces when she was a child, but now Marie was a woman and ready to fulfill her destiny.

"I thought I would take a look," said Marie. "I know you don't think it's a good idea."

"No, you are old enough now. I will not stop you. Everyone has a different experience in the mirror."

"How do you know that?"

"It's just something I know," Angela said. "But it is a private experience."

The front door opened and admitted Felicia.

"I bought some extra wine for dinner."

"That's good, we needed extra," said Angela. "Go look at the patterns, Marie. Let me know what you choose."

That night, Marie tossed to one side hoping that the change in position would trick her mind into letting go of the month's events and concerns. After an hour of staring at the wall, she walked downstairs and stood in front of her aunt's mirror. The only sound in the house was the creek in the floorboards. The hall clock tolled two a.m. She remembered counting the toll every hour when she was a child. It was the heralding of the passing of linear time, night progressing into day and day into night. Predictable and comfortable.

Marie softened her eyes and gazed into the mirror, allowing her awareness to move deeply into its vast space. Images came and went: some familiar, others undecipherable. Everything came to an abrupt halt when an image of a woman emerged from out of nowhere. She knew it was her grandmother, Speranza. She had never met her grandmother, but Angela talked about her in spirit. She did not know much about her paternal side of the family due to the circumstances surrounding Speranza's death. In the mirror, Speranza reached out with her hand, almost touching Marie's face. A peacefulness entered Marie's body, and her mind was clear.

Marie abruptly felt herself being outside the mirror. It was as if she was dreaming standing up, but the experience felt more real than a simple dream, as if she just transferred her awareness into the reality of the mirror. The dimension in the mirror was without linear time. Marie found that she could speed things up or slow them down. She touched her cheek and felt the residue of Speranza's energy, which felt warm. Speranza had stood in front of the same mirror when Angela made her clothes. Maybe the only world inside the looking glass was connected to Angela's sewing. It was easy for Marie to slide between the worlds, but she would not talk about her experiences, except to Angela. She went back upstairs and settled into bed, this time falling into a heavy sleep without dreaming.

Sunday evening, Marie was getting ready to meet Josh for their date. She put on bell-bottom jeans, a yellow blouse, and pink lipstick and walked to the West End Bar. She found Josh sitting at a small table in the back. The aroma of cigarette smoke permeated the air.

"How was your visit?"

"Better than expected."

"Really? No criticism?"

Marie settled into her chair.

"No, and when the train pulled away, my mom looked sad. That's the first time I've seen that."

"Maybe she's sad every time you leave."

"Maybe. She has been alone since my dad died, so maybe she does miss me."

As Marie listened to Josh talk about his law school classes and exams, she thought about her conversation with her aunt. She would have to stop looking outside herself for answers and listen more to the voice inside her.

"I'll go up to the bar and get us drinks. White wine ok?"

"Yes, that's fine."

Marie saw how differently she had been raised from Josh and many of her friends. Maybe it was time to celebrate it instead of pretending that she was raised like a typical American kid. She remembered the days following her father's death. The day after his death, Angela had taken Marie and Andrea to stay with her friend Catherine Calabrese, a beautiful older woman with delicate features and shiny grey hair pulled back in a bun. Angela had helped Catherine and her husband when they emigrated from Sicily many years ago, giving them furniture and a rental to get them started in America, and now it was time for her to return the favor. For three days, Angela dropped Marie and her sister off at Catherine's in the morning and picked them up in the evening. Back on Morning Glory Avenue, she brought them up the back stairway to avoid the throngs of family and friends that congregated in the dining room and the main hallway. Angela fed the girls, read them a story, and put them to bed.

Marie had not seen her mother until the reception after the funeral. She met many family members for the first time as they hugged her said how sorry they were, and that her father was a good man. It was difficult for Marie to mourn a man she felt she never knew. Angela shielded her and Andrea from other people's grief. Angela had decided that Marie and Andrea had their own relationships with Nunzio, which was not what she or what Felicia had experienced. She left it up to the young girls to decide how they would remember their father, for better or for worse.

"You just need a marketable skill if you are undecided about a career," said Josh. He placed the wine glasses down, serving Marie first.

"I guess. I'm learning a lot at the bookstore."

"I can see why your mother feels the way she does. She wants to make sure you'll be all right."

"That's comforting."

"No, I mean, you should do what you want, but she probably worries about your future, like all parents."

It was not turning out to be the romantic evening Marie had anticipated, but there was something appealing about Josh's ease and self-confidence and his obvious interest in her.

Besides, she felt the connection would ultimately be beneficial for her.

"I think we can talk about something else," said Marie, sipping her wine. "How do you like New York? Have you visited any of the sites?"

"The only site I've seen is the New York Public Library. I went there with my mom as a freshman. She can be pretty pushy."

Josh wore a black oversized sweater and a playful grin. His hair swept to one side, and his soft brown eyes jarred her memory.

"I was there that day," said Marie. "I saw you and your mom at the library. I stood next to you. I spoke to you."

Josh scratched his head.

"Really? Was that you? You were such a little girl. You're not the same person."

"No, I'm not. I was in high school. This is so strange."

"It's a coincidence," said Josh sipping his wine.

"Or destiny."

"There's no such thing. We are all just bumping into each other and there's no order to it."

"Connections are not random," Marie said.

"Agree to disagree. Do you like opera?"

"My aunt and uncle played Caruso records when I was growing up."

"This usually does not turn women on, but I have some Mozart operas at my apartment. We could go to my place and listen."

Josh touched Marie's hand and smiled. Marie found Josh attractive and was happy that he was only a few years older. Maybe her luck was changing. Now was her opportunity to engage more deeply in a relationship and let go of the fear of making a mistake. They walked out of the West End Bar hand in hand.

Josh unlocked the door of his apartment and stood back. Marie hesitated, then stepped into a dark hallway.

"The hall light is out, just walk into the living room."

"Where is the bathroom?"

"To your left."

As Marie turned on the light, a family of cockroaches scattered, running into the wall through the dingy broken white tiles. Small black and white tiles from a distant time paved the floor. Luckily, the toilet worked.

"Where are you?" asked Marie.

"In the living room."

The living room had an old chair and a TV with an antenna squatting on a crate.

"This is what Columbia gives law students. I'll be glad to get out of this dump at the end of the year."

This was a far cry from her apartment on West End Avenue. Marie and her roommate had a clean two-bedroom, first-floor apartment with a doorman and a laundry in the basement. It occurred to Marie that Manhattan housed many different levels of urban life. Some people lived in Park Avenue penthouses, others in squalid circumstances, and others who temporarily lived in run-down places but had the assurance of a much better future.

"Do you want a glass of wine?"

"No, thanks. One is enough for me."

"Let us go into the bedroom. It will be more comfortable. You know, to get away from the cockroaches. They don't seem to be in my bedroom."

Josh put on a Mozart aria, and they relaxed on the bed. He conducted the aria as if an orchestra were in front of him.

"It looks like you have conducted this before," said Marie.

"I love to feel the music. You know, in my bones."

Josh put his arm around Marie. "You are extremely cute and sexy. Men must tell you that all the time."

"Not really, but it's nice to hear."

Josh leaned in and kissed Marie. She returned the kiss in full measure and sat on Josh's lap. They undressed and slid under the covers. Josh was an involved lover, and they spent the night embracing each other and making love. At first light, Marie got dressed.

"Where are you going?" asked Josh as he rubbed his eyes.

"I have to get home and shower. I have class today, and then I have to go to work."

"Do you ever relax? I do not have a lecture until this afternoon. Why don't you hang out this morning?"

Even though Marie had skipped classes in high school, she was determined to succeed in college. High school had bored her, but she really felt she needed college in order to succeed.

Josh opened the sheets and motioned for her to come back to bed.

"I have a class at nine."

"Leave your number."

Marie leaned in, kissed Josh, then left. She walked home with the feeling that she had been too abrupt in how she left Josh. The truth was, she did not know how to sleep in. If she had missed class, she would have felt guilty all day. Still, she left Josh her number and was anxious to see him again.

Marie was getting ready to leave Brentano's for the day. A light snow was falling on Fifth Avenue, and tourists carrying packages filled the street. Salvation Army volunteers rang bells and asked for donations for the poor. She was waiting for Josh to pick her up for a stroll down Fifth Avenue.

"Marie, here is a small Christmas bonus," said the manager, handing her an envelope.

"Thanks, Jim. I appreciate it."

"Enjoy your holiday."

Josh investigated Brentano's display window and waved from the street. He wore a scarf wrapped around his neck and a wool cap pulled over his ears. Marie grabbed her coat.

"I like your scarf." Marie kissed Josh, he put his arm around her, and they began enjoying the experience of Fifth Avenue during the holiday season. They stood with the crowds in front of Saks Fifth Avenue and took in the lights. Purples, greens, and reds emanated from the window, and mannequins in Victorian dress made of lush red and gold smiled back at the people who gazed at them.

"It's such a long season," said Josh. "I feel like Christmas goes on forever. We Jews have a better way of dealing with the holidays; we ignore them."

"I think that's a great idea. But the lights are fun, especially since we're going into the dark season."

Next stop was Rockefeller Center and the mammoth tree towering over the ice-skating rink. Marie watched as the skaters went around the rink—experienced skaters, parents holding on to children, and lovers holding hands and steadying themselves against each other.

"I like the variety of skaters," said Marie. "It's like the whole world is here in this skating rink."

"Let's go into St. Patrick's Cathedral to get warm," said Josh, rubbing his hands together.

They walked slowly into the atrium, past the informational brochures and holy water fonts, and into the cathedral. The main altar was filled with poinsettias and wreaths. Visitors lit candles for lost loved ones or to have their prayers answered. The prayerful moved down the side aisles of the massive neo-gothic structure, looking up at the stained-glass windows that depicted stories from the Bible. Many poor immigrants had contributed money to the construction of the cathedral for the glory of Catholic New York in the nineteenth century. Marie wondered what the church did to thank them.

"Do you ever come here?" asked Josh.

"I am not a churchgoer. Organized religion is not my thing, but I do enjoy the art. I attended Catholic school until the eighth grade, but I found the doctrine and indoctrination stifling, to put it politely. This is the 1970s, and it's time to be our own authority."

Chapter 9
KEEP REACHING, SPRING, 1972

A s Marie's sophomore year at City College came to an end, her relationship with Josh deepened. She had decided on a history major and found that it suited her, regardless of what her mother thought. Her trips to Nelsonville became less frequent, and she was establishing her life in New York.

While walking to her job at Brentano's Books on a bright spring day, Marie wove in and out of the throngs on Fifth Avenue. Tourists speaking every romance language, German, and Arabic melded into a cacophony of sound that was energetic but grating to the ear. The languages seemed to bump up against one another to dominate; whoever spoke the loudest could rise above the rest and be heard.

She stopped in front of the Bergdorf Goodman window displaying new fashions for spring. Marie admired how the designers created their presentation. It was like a museum or gallery exhibit. She gazed at her reflection and was reminded of her aunt's warnings about staring into a mirror—but this was just clear glass. A tall, slim man appeared behind her wearing a fedora. Strange, thought Marie. Men do not wear hats anymore. There was something familiar about him, but she hesitated to turn around. She pretended to focus on the display, waiting for the man to move on. Gazing with her peripheral vision, Marie saw that he did not cast a shadow. She focused on the reflection in the window and saw that he had gone. Looking to the right and left, he was nowhere to be seen. He probably got in a cab, she thought.

When she got to work, the store was packed. The people on Fifth Avenue seemed to have piled into Brentano's.

"Excuse me, can you help me find the cooking section?" asked a customer.

"This way," said Marie. As Marie assisted the customer, she noticed a fedora peeking over the top of a shelf. Maybe this is someone else, she thought.

"Excuse me," Marie said.

She peeked around the corner but did not see the man with the fedora. Marie had not been looking into any mirrors lately, as she was just focusing on her academic work and the bookstore. But she had learned through research that the activity of gazing into a reflected object was called "scrying." It was the practice of looking into a shiny object to obtain significant messages or visions. Her aunt's warnings and her experience with her grandmother in the hall mirror had stayed with her, and she curtailed any investigation into the unseen.

"Everything all right, Marie?" asked the manager, Alister Wise.

"I am fine. I just thought I saw someone I knew."

"I wondered if you could work late tonight. We do not expect this crowd to thin out anytime soon, so if you are interested in making some extra money…"

"Sure, I'd appreciate the extra time."

Marie worked throughout the day and forgot about the man with the fedora. She connected with people from all over the globe and was amazed at the variety of their interests, from geography to biography to zoology. It was a Saturday night, and Josh was going to pick her up at nine.

"Plans for tonight?" asked Alister.

"Yeah, I'm going out for dinner."

"Before you go, would you mind helping me by standing outside while I move some books around in the window?"

Marie motioned Alister to move a display over to one side or the other. She suddenly thought she saw an outline of a form but could not distinguish what it was. She felt someone behind her.

"Are you ready to go?"

She quickly turned around. Blood filled her cheeks, and her breath deepened.

"Sorry, did I scare you?" Josh enveloped her in his arms.

Marie's face felt warm, and her palms were sweaty.

"No, let's go." Marie waved to Alister.

"I thought we would go to the Village to eat," said Josh. "I agree. It's a nice evening for the Village."

They took the subway to West 4th Street and went into a small Italian restaurant.

"How was your day?"

Marie hesitated to tell Josh about her experiences with the man in the fedora, but she thought if she spoke about it she would see that it was all a coincidence.

"You know, today I kept seeing a tall thin man wearing a fedora. He seemed so familiar."

"Was he following you?"

"I don't know. He just showed up."

"What do you mean, 'showed up'? He was either following you or he wasn't."

Josh was a realist and problem solver. There was always a practical explanation to everything in life.

"I didn't see him walk or do anything but stand behind me when I was looking into a storefront window. He did not even cast a shadow, and then I know he came to the store because I saw his fedora over a bookshelf."

"First of all, people don't just appear and disappear. He probably ended up at Brentano's because he walked down Fifth Avenue. He is probably a tourist. You have some imagination."

Marie decided not to pursue the conversation. Her sense of the situation would not resonate with Josh. Maybe she was imagining the entire scenario. If it were imaginary, then she would not see the man again. She thought she would wait and see.

After dinner, Marie and Josh strolled around Greenwich Village as he talked about his career plans, but Marie kept thinking about the man with the fedora. She noticed signs for psychics on several street corners. She had explored the Village since she was a teenager but never noticed signs for psychics or clairvoyants.

"Do you think psychics are real?" asked Marie.

"Have you been listening to me?"

"We keep passing neon signs for psychics. Do you think they are real?"

"No, I do not. You need to forget about today. It was just a coincidence."

A few weeks later, Marie was walking in Riverside Park enjoying the spring wildflowers. A cool breeze was coming off the river, and she wrapped her sweater around her chest. Twice a month she had an entire day off, and today was one of them. She had plans to walk a few miles and meet up with Josh later. The glorious weather made her feel energetic and open. She sat on a bench and watched New Yorkers pass by. It was a normal day, and life felt predictable.

"Hi, Marie, good to see you."

Marie looked up and shielded her eyes. She could not make out his face at first. She checked to make sure he cast a shadow.

"Oh, hi, Alister. Do you live around here?"

"I live downtown. I'm here giving an English lesson. I am a private tutor."

"I did not know that. You have two jobs?"

"Three, actually. I am also the buyer for Weiser Books in the Village."

"Really? I remember going to Weiser's when I was a teenager to get a book on Sufism for my brother."

Marie had been going into the city that day, and Frank had asked her to stop at Weiser's to pick up a book he had ordered. As she browsed the shop, she saw that all the titles dealt with the metaphysical. She bumped into a shelf and *The Complete Book of Witchcraft* hit her on the head.

"Did you like the shop? It's really different from Brentano's."

"It is. I did not spend much time perusing, but a book on witchcraft fell on my head."

The unseen world was not as hidden as Marie had thought. She began to understand Angela's situation of coveting her connection to the unseen. Angela had been a solo practitioner of sorts without the support of community. Regardless, she had kept her connection alive, and passed it down to Marie.

"They say when a book falls off the shelf there is something in that book you need to know. It may just be a few sentences, but there is a message or information that is important to the seeker's development."

"Seekers' development?"

"Could be an old wives' tale, but I've read some of the metaphysical books and they all say the same thing. See you at work," said Alister. "Enjoy the day."

Marie thought it was strange the memories humans file as unimportant. That day at Weiser's began to make sense to her, but she was not sure what to do next. It was time to visit Nelsonville.

When Marie arrived, Angela was ironing a skirt and blouse she'd made for Marie. She had missed their many conversations and casual time together. Angela's hands were becoming increasingly stiff from the arthritis, but she still sewed and created.

"How have you been?" asked Angela.

"Okay, I wanted to talk to you about some experiences."

Angela stopped ironing.

"I hope are not staring into mirrors. You will have trouble in your real life."

Marie told Angela about the thin man with the fedora and the witchcraft book that had fallen off the shelf. Angela put down the iron.

"Do you remember the two FBI men who came to see us about your brother?" asked Angela.

"Oh, yeah, I remember."

"Your description of the fedora man reminds me of them."

"This was different," said Marie. "He did not cast a shadow."

"That is someone without a soul," said Angela.

"Without a soul? How do you know that?"

"The old people used to say that in Sicily. Someone who was not human did not cast a shadow. You should pay attention to your studies and your life. If he shows up again, ask him what he wants to tell you then you, then decide if it is the truth."

More memories started to surface for Marie. When she was about ten years old, she had been brushing her teeth when she felt someone touch her back. She turned around quickly, only to find no one there. It was not a light touch; she had felt someone put an entire hand on her back. She was sure someone was there. Maybe these events were all connected to the mirror and seeing her grandmother.

"I used to dream about your grandmother, Speranza, all the time after she died," said Angela. "I know that she was telling me she was safe and unhappy about her husband's new marriage. Pay attention to your dreams, but do not let it get out of hand."

"It must have been lonely for you, not being able to share your beliefs."

"I have lived through an earthquake, lost my family, and been ostracized by colleagues at St. Mary's. A little loneliness will not break me. Besides, I have you. You remember what I whispered in your ear some time ago?"

"Yes. About giving up the longing to belong."

"Then follow it."

The next day, Felicia dropped Marie off at the train station.

"You know, I heard some of your conversation with Aunt Angela last night. You need to start thinking about your future and stop this nonsense about some other world. Pay attention to this one and what you will do with your life."

"You are annoying. You do not have a curious bone in your body, so you criticize others. You should be more open-minded," Marie said.

"Do not tell me what I should be! I have sacrificed for you so you could get an education and live a better life. Don't be so ungrateful."

"I am sorry, your highness, I was not aware that I owed you anything for doing your job!"

Felicia reached over to slap Marie, but she jumped out of the car and ran to the platform. The train approached the station, and Marie got on.

Marie gazed into the window of Weiser's Books. She looked around to make sure no one she knew saw her. She hadn't shared any of her experiences with anyone beside Angela and wanted to keep her personal and academic life separate from her other reality. She was dating and had been accepted into college life circles, and she wanted to keep it that way. Even though it was the 1970s in New York and people were free to be themselves, she was not sure that included metaphysical experiences. "Walk between the worlds," Aunt Angela always said. As she closed the door behind her, a bell rang, announcing her presence. The third-dimensional world faded, and she was amidst a multitude of books written about extraordinary experiences, religions, Eastern philosophy, and witchcraft.

A tall antique desk perched on a platform stood to the left, and books lined the walls from floor to ceiling.

"What brings you in?" asked the clerk sitting at the desk without looking up.

"I work with Alister at Brentano's, and he suggested I come in and look around.

"An ambitious young man," said the clerk. "What are you looking for? Maybe I can point you in the right direction." He raised his head and peered over the desk.

"Just browsing." Marie could feel his stare as she walked down one of the aisles. There were books on Sufism, magic,

Jungian psychology and the Tarot. She gingerly touched the book spines as she walked up and down the aisles.

As Marie descended one aisle toward the front of the shop, she looked toward the street and saw the tall thin man with the fedora. She froze and quickly turned toward the books. She hadn't seen him in months and thought that he must have been an apparition, but today, he appeared more three-dimensional. Marie looked up at the clerk and saw him meeting the tall thin man's gaze. The thin man left. He sees him too, she thought.

"Do you know that man?"

"He's a nuisance."

"A what?"

"A nuisance, an irritation."

"What does that mean?"

"What part of nuisance don't you understand?"

"It's just that I saw him when I was looking in a window on 5th. He didn't cast a shadow."

"Beings with compromised energy rarely cast shadows. They are fragments of a personality. This one is harmless, though."

"I don't understand."

"Why don't you check out *The Complete Book of Witch-craft* by Raymond Buckland?"

"That fell on my head once."

"You can find it in aisle three."

Marie paid for her purchase, walked onto the sidewalk, looked both ways and scurried toward the subway. The clerk had apparently sent the fedora man away. Angela had always told her to stand her ground, so the next time she saw him she would ask him what he wanted.

When she got back to her apartment, she opened her closet door and tucked the book underneath a pile of blankets. The phone rang.

"Hi, Josh. I was out for a walk. Tonight, okay. I'll meet you outside your apartment." One of the law students was giving a party, and they were invited. She would have to put on her game face and stay in physical reality. She needed to remain present, but given her recent experience, that would be a major challenge.

Marie approached Josh's apartment with a bit of trepidation. Maybe her fedora man stalker was a bored law student with an impaired sense of humor. It was said that the third year in law school was for slacking off, since most of attendance and grades had already been established. Many became bored and opened credit card tabs in bars across the city where they drank into the early hours.

"Are these your friends?" asked Marie.

"They're just acquaintances. We're all in competition with each other for grades and jobs."

"So, you don't like each other."

"Not really. The guy who is giving the party just got a coveted lobbyist job in Washington, D.C. He wants to show off."

"Sounds like a great life."

Josh looked at Marie.

"We're all a part of the same club. Graduating from Columbia Law School opens doors. Maybe not as quickly for a Harvard graduate, but pretty close."

Josh's life was guaranteed whether he wanted to follow that path or not; it was predictable and stable. Marie realized that his challenges in life would be easily traversed, so his learning curve would be low. He would most likely be the same in twenty years, with little growth or development.

The party was populated with first, second, and third-year law students munching on chips, dip, and cheap wine. Marie had expected shrimp and foie gras from a Columbia soiree. What they lacked in culinary taste, they made up for in university prestige.

"Come in, Josh," said a young man with a Columbia Law School sweatshirt.

"Aaron, this is Marie."

"Oh, yeah, Josh has told me about you. Come in and grab a drink."

Marie never really enjoyed parties, but she was trying to be more social.

"Congrats, Aaron, on your new job," said Josh. "I'm sure you'll be successful."

"Thanks. So, when did you two meet?"

"We met several years ago at the New York Public Library. And again recently at Brentano's."

"Really? That's fate for you," said Aaron as he sipped his beer.

"Marie thinks it's some cosmic connection," said Josh, "instead of coincidence, which it is."

"My aunt would say there were no coincidences or accidents," said Marie.

"Then what?" asked Aaron. "There are no accidents? We call them accidents for a reason."

"Accidents happen to steer people in a different direction. There is an order and balance to everything."

"This is way too deep for me," said Josh. "We're at a party."

Marie met some of the few female law students and observed that they had similar ambitions to their male counterparts, but it was obvious the men would get the most coveted jobs. They all dated each other, all locked into a predictable future, and the worst part was they didn't question their choices. Any anxiety Marie had about not knowing what she would do with her life began to melt, and she was grateful that her future was open and not decided by a profession that would treat her unfairly. Her future was wide open.

"Don't you think there is more to life than just good grades and a job at the end of your third year?" asked Marie to a woman in her third year who had not secured a job yet.

"Like what?"

"There's experiencing life on a different level. Look around you, there is always mystery and exploring the unknown."

"All that doesn't pay the bills or get your kids into the best schools. That's fantasy and excuses for doing poorly in life."

"I wish you luck."

"Ready to go?" asked Josh.

"So soon?"

'Yeah, I see these people a lot. And besides, I'm tired of Aaron gloating. His grades aren't even as good as mine."

"Don't you think this competition is a waste of time?"

"No, it's what we do. Keeps us motivated."

Marie had an innate sense of the unseen world and its possibilities and knew that it was never a good idea to get involved in someone else's petty concerns. She would find out who the fedora man was and why he followed her. He did not feel threatening or dangerous and was easily sent away by the clerk at Weiser's Books.

"Want to meet up tomorrow?"

"I have to work. It's Saturday."

Josh put his arm around Marie as they walked back to his apartment.

Saturday was consistently busy at Brentano's, especially in good weather. Alister came in and began to open the register.

"Hi, Alister, glad you're here today."

"Marie, how are you?"

"I went to Weiser's Books."

"How did it go?"

"You are an amazing buyer."

"I can't take all the credit. Some of those titles have been there for years."

"The clerk is a character," Marie said.

"Oh, you met Bartholomew. I think he came with the place; he's been there for so long."

"He sent away a man that was following me. He sent him away just by meeting his gaze."

"Maybe he was one of the indigents in the neighborhood and Bartholomew was used to dealing with him."

"Bartholomew said he was a compromised being and that's why he didn't cast a shadow," said Marie.

"Leave it to him to come up with a story like that."

At the end of the day, Marie rearranged books on the front table and looked toward 5th Avenue. Someone waved from the street; it was Uncle Joe. Marie motioned for him to come in.

"Hello, Darling. I thought we could have an early dinner if you're not busy."

"That is a great idea. I'm done for the day."

They went into a small Italian restaurant known for its hearty home-style meals, not far from 5th Avenue.

"So, how is everything?" Joe asked as he spun his spaghetti around his fork.

"Good. I'm enjoying my classes and my job."

"New York can be a tough place to live. I spoke with Aunt Angela today. She misses you."

"Yeah, I call her during the day sometimes to make sure she's okay. I'll make a trip soon to Nelsonville."

"Your mother is concerned about you, but I said that you'll be fine."

"You're right. I will be."

"You were such a shy little girl. I see that you've changed. New York will do that to you."

"I've learned that I can live on my own, so I'm not reliant on anyone. I can make my own way."

"I know, but your mother is concerned that you won't have a stable life. You should start thinking about a stable career and marriage."

Marie felt that her uncle was pleading her mother's case and that his concern was not genuine. Maybe Felicia felt that two people making a compelling case was better than one. The difference between her mother, Joe and Angela was that Angela was confident that Marie would be fine regardless of her choices.

"I'm nineteen and living in New York. I'm in college and I have a job, so I would say that I'm doing really well and don't need anyone to keep tabs on me."

"Oh, I'm not doing that," said Joe.

"You mean my mother didn't ask you to stop by the store and take me to dinner?"

"I'm not spying, if that's what you think."

Marie looked at her uncle with raised eyebrows.

"All right, all right, she asked me to see how you were doing. I love your mother and I don't like her to worry."

"So, you weren't worried about me."

"Honey, if you're anything like your mother and aunt, you'll do better than fine. I could not say no to your mother when she asked me to check on you. I can tell her that I did as she asked. You know your mama."

"You don't have to tell me."

"I'm not educated, but I know how important it is for Angela and your mother that you graduate college. Anything else going on? How about boys?"

"I'm seeing someone, if that's what you're asking."

"Well, do tell. I'm all ears."

"I don't want this to get to mom."

"Your secret is safe with me."

"Really?"

"No, but I am interested."

"He's someone I met at work; a law student."

"Kudos to you," Joe said. "Do I hear wedding bells?"

"I'm supposed to finish college, remember?"

Marie recognized that Joe meant well, but he functioned on one level of existence: the material plane. Gucci shoes, Armani suits and vacations on the French Riviera or anything that would bring him status was his desire. These accoutrements of New York wealth enabled him to feel superior to his contemporaries who did not fare as well. It eased the neglect he had experienced as a child.

"How is Dick?"

"At the moment he's in L.A. negotiating a deal. I have a lot of free time while he's away. Why don't I call your mother and we can all have lunch?"

"You really love her."

"She has been good to me. Did you know she sent me money so I could attend her wedding to my brother? She knew I had no money, and she wanted me there. I have never forgotten that. She made me feel like I was part of the family."

"No, I didn't know."

"So, if I'm on her side, I have my reasons. We are both from immigrant families and experienced our parents' difficulties in assimilating. Some bonds can't be broken."

Joe paid the check, and they walked out onto the street. There was a lull in activity before New Yorkers descended on the sidewalks, crowding into restaurants and going to the theater.

"I'll invite your mother for lunch next week. We can all get together."

Marie kissed Joe goodbye and walked toward the subway. She stood on the platform, leaned against a beam, and contemplated the relationship between her family members. Angela's influence and relationship with family members was clear. She shared her history with everyone, and they respected her. Marie knew Angela intimately—her hardships, hopes and dreams—but she only knew other family members superficially. They were superfluous to her past, and in her mind irrelevant to her future.

Marie turned and noticed the edge of a black hat peeking out from behind the adjacent beam. Her heart began to race as the image of the man with the fedora flooded her mind. She hid behind the beam and made her body stiff, deciding not to board the oncoming train. As the train left the station, she slowly peered around the beam. Whoever it was, he had boarded the train.

Marie slept fitfully that night, and between waking and sleep she thought about the thin man with the fedora. Maybe he reflected the hidden part of herself and was trying to get her attention. She got up and retrieved the book she had purchased at Weiser's Books. The contents included the history and philosophy of witchcraft, divination methods, herbal lore, and dream interpretation. She read until the early morning and then fell into a deep sleep.

Angela was dusting the lion statue on her mantle when the phone rang.

"Marie, how are you doing?"

"I'm good, Aunt Angela. How are you?"

"Oh, I am old, so I do my best. When are you coming for a visit?"

"Soon."

"Your uncle told me told me you had dinner together. He seemed to think I did not know you have a boyfriend."

"He's just someone I see. I'm not sure he's my boyfriend. I wanted to tell you I saw the man with the fedora again. It's getting really strange."

There was a pause at the end of the phone.

"You must ask him what he wants."

"That's what I thought, but why is this happening? You don't seem surprised that this is happening."

Marie heard Angela take a deep breath.

"I have had encounters with this kind of being. Once, after the earthquake when I went back to my home, he was there trying to get me to go with him, but I did not. He seemed underhanded and not of this earth. It doesn't seem like your man is out to harm you."

"No, I don't think he is. I will be home in a few weeks."

"I hope you do come. I have something for you. We can talk some more when you visit. Aren't you having lunch with your uncle and mother next week?"

"Yes, I suppose I will go. It's never that interesting."

"Then make it go your way."

Angela hung up and went into her bedroom. She took out her diamond earrings that Franco had given her on their tenth anniversary. The diamonds were oval shaped in a silver setting imported from Palermo. She felt it was time to give them to Marie. She felt she was coming to the end of her journey and wanted to begin the letting go process. The doctor said that she was in good health, but life was unpredictable, and she believed in preparedness. She had not worn them much, just on special occasions. They had spent years sitting in her drawer, and it was time that they were out in the world.

Angela thought about Marie's ability to move to Manhattan at age eighteen on her own and create a life for herself. Angela had made the trip from Sicily to America, but that was with a husband and a family waiting for her. She saw Marie's journey as more difficult, given the changes in American culture. She saw how her influence had given Marie her desire to take on a challenge like living in New York City. She recognized Marie's gift to connect to the occult world, but how that would be revealed was different for everyone. She put the earrings away and lit the candles on her altar. Angela wondered if when she died she could come back to the physical world and be with her family. Given her adept communication with the unseen world, maybe she could connect with the living, like she did with her unseen friends. Life carries on, she thought. It does not end when the last breath is taken.

Marie brushed her long, thick, dark hair from her scalp to its ends. She was on her way to meet Joe and her mother for dinner and decided to create a French braid so she would look more sophisticated. Joe had wanted to go to a new trendy restaurant in Greenwich Village, so he had changed the time from lunch to dinner. She wore a form- fitting black dress with a V neckline, and black pumps topped off the outfit. The restaurant was near Weiser's Books, so she had decided to meet them at the restaurant.

She walked down 4th Avenue and gazed into the Weiser's Books window. The window display consisted of several volumes about Sufism, including *The Essential Rumi* and *The Garden of Truth: The Vision and Promise of Sufism*. Bartholomew was perched on his high chair overseeing the activity below. It was a Friday evening, and the shop was crowded with the local intelligentsia and spiritual seekers. She felt she was among the spiritual seekers who wanted to know more about the occult world and how it interfaced with the physical plane. The shop was open until 11 pm on Friday evenings, so she decided to return after dinner.

Marie found Joe and Felicia sitting at a round table in a quiet corner of the restaurant. There were brass chandeliers hanging from dark wooden beams, and white taper candles lit at each table with white tablecloths and matching napkins.

"There she is," said Joe, lifting his martini.

"I don't know why you did not take a cab with us," Felicia said. "Did you take the subway?"

"Part of the way. I got off at 42nd Street and walked the rest of the way." Marie sat down and placed a napkin on her lap.

"You're here, it doesn't matter how," said Joe. "Take a look at the menu, Marie. The cuisine is a fusion of American, Italian, and French, very in now." Joe was dressed in a cream cashmere turtleneck, embellished with a gold chain and black slacks.

"What's new, everyone?" Marie asked.

"Your mother and I may go dancing after dinner," Joe said.

"Sounds exciting."

"There used to be dance halls where people could go, but no more. Remember that, Joe? I so enjoyed that."

"I remember. You see, Marie, we both married stick-in-the-muds, but we have had each other."

Marie saw her mother smile, and the genuine affection between the pair emerged. They were content in each other's company because of their shared history.

"Yes, we have," said Felicia.

"I admire your mother. She is a strong woman; a survivor."

Felicia smiled, and she seemed happy. Marie thought her mother had not received much positive reinforcement throughout the years and when she did receive it, she lit up. Marie usually resented it when they excluded her from the conversation, but now the resentment faded and she understood how important their relationship was to their well-being.

"You are a survivor, too," Felicia said to Joe. "We have that in common, and we have a friendship that will extend into the future."

"I will drink to that," said Marie, lifting her wine glass. "To Felicia and Joe, the dynamic duo who climbed many mountains, supported one another, and came out the other side stronger."

"Thank you, Marie," said Felicia. "I am glad you acknowledge that." She rubbed Marie's shoulder, and she and Joe smiled at one another.

"Now this is good," said Joe.

"Can I get anyone another drink?" asked the waitress.

"I love your earrings," Joe said. "They're a nice touch."

"Thanks," the waitress said as she touched her ears. "It's nice of you to notice."

"I notice everything, and I can tell you have style." Joe smiled at the waitress and she turned pink. "I would like another martini."

"I will have another highball," said Felicia.

Marie limited herself to one glass of wine, and she never drank hard liquor. As her dinner companions sipped their drinks, laughed and relaxed, she began to feel she was part of the conversation and sat back to listen. Even though she did not say much, she felt they were sharing their relationship with her, presenting who they were years ago and how their relationship evolved.

"Marie, I always told your mother that she should remarry, but she did it her way and I have to say she was right."

"I'm glad you see it my way," Felicia said. "It was best for my career and my children. I was able to be the mother I wanted to be."

"I would say you two have a lot to celebrate," said Marie.

They finished the evening with tiramisu and espresso. The threesome strolled onto the sidewalk and talked about the rampant crime and economic collapse that had gripped the city.

"In the 1960s, the city was full of life and diversity," Joe said as he lit a cigarette. "Now buildings are collapsing, and there is not money to fix them. Dick and I have even talked about moving to London."

"I am sure it will improve," Marie said. "New York always survives."

"You'll visit next weekend?" Felicia asked.

"Yes, Aunt Angela said there was something she wanted to give me. I'm due for a visit anyway."

"Always nice to have you home," said Felicia.

Marie stopped and watched as her mother and uncle walked ahead. She never got the impression that her mother was even remotely pleased with her visits. Her statement was completely out of character.

"Are you coming?" asked Felicia. "We're taking a cab uptown."

Joe and Felicia stopped and looked at Marie. This was her legacy, she thought.   Martinis, highballs, and long-term relationships based on like minds and experiences. Joe hailed a cab, and they sped uptown.

Marie and Angela finished lunch and put the dishes in the sink.

"I'm glad you could come this weekend," Angela said. "I have something for you. I think it's the right time."

"What is it?"

"Come in the bedroom."

Angela's bedroom felt smaller, and the pink bedspread with embroidered flowers Marie remembered as a child was draped over the bed like a relic.

"I wanted to give you these before I pass away." She handed Marie the earrings.

"They're beautiful," said Marie. "But are you sure? You might want to wear them."

"No, I want you to enjoy them. Diamonds increase intuition and imagination, and you will benefit from them."

"Thank you, Aunt Angela." She put her arms around Angela and held her tight.

"So, tell me about this mysterious man you have been seeing," Angela prompted.

"Like I said, he wears a fedora. I went to Weiser's Books, and I saw him outside gazing in the window. The shopkeeper said he did not cast a shadow because he had no soul. He made him leave just by staring at him."

"These strange people show up when we have to look at a part of ourselves that has been lost. Some are benevolent, others malevolent. Your man seems harmless, but he does have a message. When did you last see him?"

"At a subway stop not too long ago, but I hid."

"He won't go away until you confront him. I think you should."

"It's so strange how all this has transpired. I'm so glad you're here to help me."

"One day I won't be."

Marie felt a chill. When she imagined a future without Angela, she saw confusion and indecision. Angela had been with Marie since birth, and one day she would be gone.

"You will have many more years," said Marie.

"You never know when God will call me, so it is best to be prepared. Besides, I will never really leave you. You have to know that by now, or is your education telling you that you cannot trust what you don't see?"

Marie thought about the fedora man and realized that he might be that part of her that doubted her ability to connect with the unseen world—that she had been concentrating on school, work, and her relationship with Josh, who was focused on intellect.

"You had told me to be careful with whom I shared my intuition, so I have been fitting in."

"But I did not tell you to reject it."

"I am not rejecting my intuition. I'm just keeping it quiet for a while." Marie knew she needed to clear up the mystery of the fedora man so she could move on with her life.

"All right," said Angela, "we all have to make choices, and right now you have made yours."

M arie climbed into her old bed at Morning Glory Avenue and drifted off into a subterranean sleep; the kind of sleep that allows a body to completely let go and rest. She found herself standing by her bed looking down at her body. Suddenly she found herself on a street in an old city.

She was not sure where she was or what she was supposed to do. All she could think was that she needed to get back to her body, but then she thought that maybe she was supposed to explore this strange landscape and walk along its streets and avenues. The street signs were in French, and the buildings were centuries old. She continued down one narrow street. There were people in shops chatting with shop owners.

Although she could not hear them, she could understand what they were saying. They whispered about all the killings and talked about who was taken away. The women wore simple long dresses. and the men were dressed in black with long pants. Marie recalled taking a course on French history in college. During the French Revolution, people were forced to dress alike to dissolve the distinction between aristocrat and commoner. Silks and ruffles were forbidden, and men had to wear long pants. Marie did not understand why she was experiencing this. She moved to the next shop.

A few doors down, a shoemaker, alone in his shop, seemed to be in a hurry as he worked, but occasionally he would look up at the window where Marie stood and stare. Did he know she was there? Marie lifted her finger and tapped on the glass. The shoemaker did not look up from his work. This is just a dream. This isn't real. He can't see me. Then Marie realized that it was her dream, and her creation, and she could speak to anyone she wanted. A bell rang as she closed the shop door.

"Excuse me, sir, I don't speak French; do you speak English?" Marie moved closer to the shoemaker.

"If you would like me to," said the shoemaker.

"My name is Marie. I'm from New York, in America." She held out her hand.

"I know who you are," said the cobbler. He looked up and smiled.

She expected him to have a ghostly presence, but he had reddish cheeks and clear eyes.

"Can you tell me where I am?"

"Paris, of course. 1789."

"But why? Why am I here?"

The cobbler put down his tools. "You are like my customers. You never ask the right question."

"What is the right question?"

"I'll tell you when you ask it," said the shoemaker. "What date is it where you come from?"

"It's 1972," said Marie.

"Much change must be happening in your world." He began to polish one of his shoes. "There must be increased interest in metaphysics and the spiritual realm."

"Yes, it seems so. How do you know?"

"I am a seer. I read people from their shoes. Nothing is more revealing than how we walk through life; I read the imprint. But I will die for my crime of using my intuition and exploring the spiritual realm to help people heal. You are extremely fortunate, Marie. Take advantage of all the opportunities that will come your way. This is just the beginning. The 1970s will be a tremendous time for change. Find out about your history." He picked up a broom and began to sweep.

"Really? Why?"

The shoemaker turned to respond, but Marie awoke and looked around the room. Sun streamed in through the stained-glass window. An entire night had passed in a flash, and she felt like she had jumped through time and back. It came to her that what the shoemaker meant was to research the history of people who had made the exploration of the spiritual realm their life's work.

Marie sat in the New York Public Library perusing books on the French Revolution. She looked for the revolution's treatment of seers and psychic readers but could find nothing. The tarot had been around since the Middle Ages in Europe, so she was sure there had to have been readers in Paris during the eighteenth century—but she could find no historical documentation. She left the library and went to Weiser's Books to continue her research. She found a small book on the history of psychic readers and fortune-tellers in Europe. The author made the following statement:

"I don't believe we can ever know what happened to the seers during the Middle Ages. They were hunted, tortured, and burned as witches. I am sure many survived and continued their work, secretly passing down their wisdom and knowledge to others. Even though France was a Catholic country, Paris was a refuge for displaced psychics and intuitives, much like the expressionist painters in the nineteenth century."

The writer went on to say that the readers blended into Parisian society and worked in practical professions that allowed them to use their talents. He quoted a woman named Madame Beaumarches, who kept a detailed diary of her experience while imprisoned in the Bastille. She talked about a shoemaker who had been instrumental in helping her deal with her life. She said he was the kindest man she had ever met and that he offered accurate insight into her life when he held her shoes.

"The shoemaker would hold my shoes as if holding a newborn child, and then, as if in a trance, he would talk until no more information would come forth. My life would have been much more difficult without him, and I am sure others have had the same experience. I am eternally grateful for his council."

Marie slowly lowered herself onto a stool next to the bookshelf. Could it be possible that she had encountered the shoemaker in her dream, or was reading shoes commonplace for seers in Paris? She had reached across what is perceived as linear time while in a dream state. History is there for everyone to touch, she thought, and nothing is fixed in time. She thought of herself as someone who might have survived witch hunts and used her intuitive skills while working in a different profession, which meant she had lived before. She was just at the beginning of her journey, but she could now embark on her quest with an awareness that would light her way.

She brought the book to Bartholomew to purchase it.

"You're back," said the clerk, "and so is your friend."

Marie turned to the street and saw the fedora man standing near the door.

"Guess I should talk with him and hear what he has to say."

"Not the worst idea," Bartholomew said.

"Do you think it is safe? I mean, he is following me and he's strange-looking."

"You're not special. Many people are followed by their shadow; you just happen to have manifested yours. Takes skill, but not special."

"I could be harmed," said Marie. "That's a cavalier attitude."

"Like I said, not special; it's just the next step. I would like to take care of the next customer."

Marie stepped out onto the street holding the book to her chest, and she looked up at the tall man. She felt her diminutive size as she stretched to look into his eyes.

"Why are you following me?"

"That's the big question, isn't it? I would surmise that you need to get on your path. All that time your aunt spent preparing you, and yet it has taken a back seat."

"What has taken a back seat?"

"I don't know why you need to ask that question, but all right. To communicate with the world that nobody sees. Humans are scrambling around, walking through souls that are begging to be recognized. Shame, really."

"How do you know about my aunt?"

"We have followed her since the earthquake in 1908 to make sure she maintained her connection with the unseen world, and then she shared it with you."

"Now what?"

"Now you make your choice. I am here to remind you to embrace your intuition and pull back from the linear path you are on. You do not want to live a soulless life, and if you keep negating your intuition and psychic talent, then you will feel soulless. Keep investigating and see where it takes you. At any rate, I have done my job. I wish you luck." He turned to walk away.

"Wait a minute. Who are you?"

"That's not important, but I will tell you I am old—older than you can imagine—and I have followed you through lifetimes."

"Will I see you again?" called Marie, but the man had disappeared.

The events of the past weeks had catapulted Marie into a new beginning. The patterns in her life emerged as connected energies with different paths and timelines. The choice was now hers. She knew the choice needed to be made through her connection with herself, and from a space of confidence.

Marie walked along 5th Avenue on her way to Brentano's to work her shift. She looked around for the tall man with the fedora, telling herself that she should be frightened with her strange encounters, but she was not. Through her aunt, she had had many unusual experiences in front of the mirror; experiences that most people would consider made up, but now she was sure they were valuable and real.

"Hi, Alister," Marie said.

"Hi, haven't seen you in a while. What have you been doing?"

"It's been a bucket of weird."

"Weird is good. Better than boredom, and sometimes weird helps us clarify who we are."

"You know, I think you're right," said Marie. "I'll begin to shelve the new titles."

Marie decided that she would become her own authority and not listen to the opinion of others. She had had enough of being told she should tiptoe around authority figures so that she would not create waves, intentionally slipping through the cracks so that part of her would be hidden from others. Life would be different from now on.

Marie dialed the number in Nelsonville, knowing her aunt would be the only one home in the middle of the day.

"The fedora man said that I need to follow my intuition more. That is what his appearance has been about. He said I was becoming more linear and could lose who I really am and feel lost regardless of what I achieve."

"His observation was accurate," Angela said.

"I'm not sure what that will look like, but I'll try."

"If anyone can succeed, you can. When will you be visiting?"

"I'm not sure. I'll let Mom know. See you soon."

"I love you, Marie. You have been a gift to me."

"I love you."

Marie sat on her bed and flipped through Buckland's *Complete Book of Witchcraft*, wondering about her next step. She had continued to see Josh, but she felt herself withdrawing from the relationship. Keeping part of her life hidden from him had created a barrier. He did not notice, but Marie did. She edited her life so that the relationship could continue without disagreement or friction. Any answers she needed she would not find in a book. She just had to be herself and believe that was enough. Josh had accepted a position of a clerk for a judge in New York City, and even though Marie did not see herself as part of that world, she was not ready to let it go.

Chapter 10
REVELATIONS
FALL 1972

Marie and Angela walked along the streets in Nelsonville glancing in store windows. Angela was using a cane to steady herself, as her balance had become compromised in the last few months.

"What will you do after college?" Angela said. "You should think ahead."

"You sound like Mom."

"It doesn't hurt to think about things."

"The next step would be graduate school, but I may choose a different path."

"You can choose whatever path you want, just choose one. Do you still have your boyfriend?"

"Yes, he's clerking for a judge in New York."

"Is he important to you?"

"I guess he is, but I don't share what you and I talk about."

"So, he doesn't know about your experiences?"

Marie did not have the fortitude to break it off. Her relationship with Josh made her feel part of the world in a concrete way.

"No, but that's okay. I am satisfied with where the relationship is right now. I'm walking between the worlds."

"If anyone can do that, it's you," Angela said. "I'm sure your mother would like to meet him. You should bring him to see us one weekend."

"I could do that, but I think he would find Nelsonville old-fashioned."

"You mean he would find me old."

"I think he will find you exotic. And you're not old at seventy-seven."

Marie put her arm around Angela as they sauntered toward Morning Glory Avenue. It was a sunny fall day, and the leaves were changing into brilliant oranges and yellows. The brisk autumn breeze reminded Marie of her moving day to New York City two years before. The day she moved she had started her life, and prior to that she felt she was marking time.

"I did not think this town could serve your needs," Angela said.

"How so?"

"When you were a little girl, you wanted to know all about New York and who lived there. You loved your Uncle Joe's stories even when you were three years old."

"Really?"

"I think you always knew what you wanted. You knew where you wanted to be."

Marie thought that maybe Angela was right but that she had just taken detours to please others and fit in. She had experienced flashes of insight about where she wanted to be as a child, including her attraction to New York City and other worldly experiences, and when it came times to choose, she chose to follow her flashes.

"I just followed the flashes I had about my future. I think it was my intuition bleeding into my everyday life. They felt like possibilities, and through your support I explored those possibilities."

"Glad you see that. Do you need anything before you go back to the city? Do you have everything you need?"

"Yes, I have everything."

"Don't forget to bring your boyfriend the next time you come home. We all want to meet him."

O ne Saturday morning, Marie and Josh boarded the train to Nelsonville at Grand Central Station.

"My family is different from yours," Marie said.

"All families are the same," Josh said.

Josh had a penchant for critical analysis. It was also important for him to be around materially successful people. He had never even pondered the possibility of an unseen world or an intuitive approach to life.

"I wouldn't say that. My family immigrated to this country not long ago, so their attitude toward life stems from that point in time."

"Are we going to talk about hardship and the American experience? Do they rehash the past?"

"Sometimes, but when they do they put a different spin on it. They know how to turn any negative encounter around, and they do not mince words."

"I look forward to meeting them."

"Great. Keep that in mind."

M arie and Josh walked toward Felicia's car.

"Mom, this is Josh."

"Josh, it's so nice to meet you," Felicia said. "I've heard a lot about you. You're a lawyer?"

"Guilty."

"I work with a lot of lawyers. In my experience, some of them just don't know what they're doing."

"I don't disagree. I'm clerking right now, but I will probably go into teaching."

"That would be a stable career; smart move. I'm hoping Marie will make the same smart choice."

Josh smiled at Marie, pleased that he had found common ground with Felicia right out of the gate.

"I always encourage her to decide on a stable career."

"You do?"

On the short ride, they mostly talked about Josh's developing career. Angela was waiting on the porch as they ascended the stairs.

"Marie, so glad to see you," said Angela. She hugged Marie and kissed her on each cheek. "And this is your boyfriend."

"It's nice to meet you all. I wish I could say I know a lot about you, but Marie seldom talks about her family."

"Ask us anything you want," Angela said. "We can get to know each other that way."

"It's just the four of us this weekend," Felicia said, "so we'll have plenty of time to get to know one another."

Marie suddenly felt trapped and exposed. She had presented herself one way to Josh and had not revealed the true influences in her formative years. She took a deep breath and prepared to embrace the journey.

"We have made lasagna for tonight," Angela said.

For new guests, Angela would serve basic, traditional Italian dishes that were familiar to Americans, like spaghetti and meatballs.

"I love lasagna," said Josh.

After they had settled into their respective rooms, Josh found Angela in the kitchen.

"So, you helped raise Marie and her siblings."

"Me and their mother. Their father, Nunzio, died many years ago."

"It's nice that your family pulled together after he died. I did not have turmoil in my upbringing. Anything I wanted, I got."

"That doesn't mean you had a healthy upbringing," Angela said.

"There you are," Marie said. "I thought we'd go for a walk before dinner."

"Your aunt and I were getting acquainted."

"We can do that at dinner," said Marie.

Marie and Josh left through the side door. Angela thought Josh had presented himself as stable and responsible, but she wondered how he would feel about Marie as she revealed more of herself.

Marie and Josh walked hand in hand toward town. She could tell he was uncomfortable with the provincial atmosphere of Nelsonville. They came up to an old church with a playground surrounded by chains.

"This is the Catholic school I went to, up until the eighth grade."

"It's like something out of a sit-com. Now I understand why you are the way you are. I mean, that house you grew up in. It's no wonder you have trouble staying in the present, all of this is a blast from the past."

"What do you mean?"

"It's just an observation."

"Are you saying I don't fit into the modern world?"

"I'm saying this town is steeped in the past, and it is unsophisticated. I'm surprised you got out."

Marie released Josh's hand and moved away. It was not surprising to Marie that she had left Nelsonville. She finally saw Josh's limited vision—not only toward her, but himself. He would be content teaching in a law school, buying a house, and living an upper middle-class life. Her vision extended past that into the unseen world and beyond. Josh saw the physical world as the only reality.

"Where do you want to live in the future?" Marie asked.

"Wherever my career takes me, so I can move up in my career."

"I would not move around for a career. I would choose a place I loved and build a career there."

"That's the difference between us," Josh said.

"Let's go back," Marie said. "They'll be waiting for us."

"I am enjoying this lasagna," Josh said. "I was telling Marie today that I was surprised she got out of this town. It's the kind of town that grips people for life."

"Felicia and I both encouraged the children to reach past Nelsonville," Angela said. "Isn't that right, Felicia?"

"New York has been a great resource for us," Felicia said.

"I imagine Marie would have lived a mundane life had she stayed in Nelsonville," Josh said.

"Marie would never live a mundane life, no matter where she lived," Angela said. "That would not be possible."

"How do you know that?" Josh asked.

"I would say that she expands her mind and uses her intuition."

At the beginning of dinner, Marie had hoped the conversation would not go in this direction, but after her interaction with Josh earlier she was happy to let the discussion go where it needed. It was inevitable that Josh would find out about her predilection toward the occult world, so it was best to finally expose who she was.

"I always thought she should pay more attention to daily happenings, rather than indulge in fantasy," Felicia said. "She has a tendency to do that, but I think with your influence she will be more practical."

Marie felt she was as unseen as the invisible world. This was an opportunity for her to be who she was, and either be accepted or rejected.

"I do not indulge in fantasy," Marie said. "I just add to the physical world through connecting with the unseen."

"You can't believe you actually contact other realities," Josh said.

"I've done it my entire life."

Marie took a deep breath and felt the words roll uncontrollably off her tongue. Retraction was not an option.

"I told you," said Felicia, shaking her head. "Fantasy."

Angela felt she should say something but decided to let Marie take the lead.

"There isn't just this reality, there are a zillion others—too many to count. So, I don't live my life only in the physical; that would be far too confining."

Marie looked around and waited for a response. Time, which Marie had regarded as a nebulous concept, froze as she felt Josh and Felicia's fixed stares.

"To each their own," said Josh, "but I happen to know that this is the only reality that matters."

"How do you know?" Marie asked.

"Because if I can't see it, it does not exist," Josh said. "I have enough issues with this reality. I don't need more."

"I agree with you," Felicia said. "Who needs more problems?"

"That does not mean the occult world is not there."

"How do you know it is?" Josh asked.

Angela felt that this conversation was long overdue. It was necessary before Josh and Marie became more serious about their relationship, but now she saw that their romance would face a huge challenge.

"Because I have experienced it. Isn't that right, Aunt Angela?"

"You know that I have experienced the unseen world firsthand and that you have the gift. I wonder, Josh, why are you so against communication with the other side?"

"This is ridiculous," Felicia said. "I'll serve the dessert."

"What have you experienced that I don't know about?" Josh asked. "I guess I don't know you that well, since you don't really share your life."

"I've met beings no longer on the earth plane and also met someone who didn't have a shadow because he didn't have a soul."

"Marie!" said Felicia. "Let's talk about something else."

Marie felt a weight lift from her mind, knowing she no longer would have to choose her words carefully so she would not offend someone. She would not have to negate her experiences or who she was. The rest of the meal was spent talking superficially about New York City and all the changes taking place. Marie was shocked that she just declared herself, for all intents and purposes, a witch—and that everyone simply had moved on.

Josh and Marie rode the train back to Manhattan in heavy silence. Regardless of the state of their relationship, Marie had been authentic, and that had brought her an uncomfortable peace. It would be impossible going forward to hide and pretend that she was someone else. Concealing who she was would no longer work, but being herself would have its consequences, both positive and negative. She would have to embrace both. She needed to break the ice with Josh.

"Maybe we should take a break from one another," Marie said. "I know that was a lot to take in."

"I was thinking the same thing. We are so different, and we don't have much in common. I don't agree with your beliefs."

"They're not beliefs, they're my personal internal experience. I am open to other points of view. I am not as rigid as you in your opinions."

"I am entitled to my opinions, but what you're espousing is beyond simple opinion, and most people would find it unsettling. Your mother does, but your aunt has obviously had a major influence on you."

Josh turned and stared out at the passing landscape. The train pulled into Grand Central Station, and they stepped onto the platform.

"I'm going to stop and see a friend," Josh said, "so I'm not going straight home. I'll give you a call."

Marie watched as Josh walked away, becoming smaller and smaller as he slipped into the crowd and disappeared. She thought that she should call after him and say that she would not keep exploring the unseen and that the physical world was enough for her, but that would be a lie.

She was sad that she had lost the relationship, but relieved that she was finally free to be herself. It seemed that the platform at Grand Central Station had been a stage for her family to play out dramas, as it was the link connecting the suburb community in Nelsonville to the intensity and richness of New York City. Marie resolved that it was time for her to embrace her future in Manhattan.

She remembered what Angela had whispered to her years ago, "Give up the longing to belong."

About the Author

C armela Cattuti stated her writing career as a writer for the Somerville News in Boston, MA. She is a writer, painter, and yoga instructor in Boston. After she finished her graduate work in English Literature at Boston College, she began to write creatively and taught journal writing at the Cambridge Center for Adult Education. As fate would have it, she felt compelled to write her great-aunt's story. *Between the Cracks* and *The Ascent* are the first two novels in the series. This is the third in the trilogy.

To connect with Carmela, email her at cattutic@gmail.com or visit her web site, www.ccattuticreative.com.

Made in United States
North Haven, CT
11 April 2023

35318653R00121